A Look
In The Mirror

A Look
In The Mirror

Terrence LeRoy Baker

authorHOUSE®

AuthorHouse™
1663 Liberty Drive
Bloomington, IN 47403
www.authorhouse.com
Phone: 833-262-8899

Published by AuthorHouse 11/16/2023

ISBN: 978-1-4969-0366-2 (sc)
ISBN: 978-1-4969-0367-9 (hc)
ISBN: 978-1-4969-0368-6 (e)

Library of Congress Control Number: 2014906956

Printed in the United States of America

1-27-24

Victoria

Thanks for being too

[signature]

PROLOGUE

I remember when I went on my first date. Not the typical date, like going to the movies or a school dance. No, this was with a crackhead friend of my mother. She just so happened to be gone down the street to get her medicine—at least, that's what she called it, but we knew medicine came in bottles, not plastic sandwich bags.

I was only eleven years old when it happened, which is no excuse, because I knew exactly what I was doing. I may not have known anything about condoms or giving head, but it wasn't as hard as I would've thought. He only gave me five dollars, but it was cool—he also went to McDonald's and got me, my baby sister Jackie, and my older brother Carlton breakfast meals. At first I thought I would feel shame or guilt, but actually, it made me feel good. Life was rough for all of us—so rough that none of us went to school.

We lived in an abandoned building where there was no running water, no heat, and no lights. The building seemed to have been burned to the ground before because it smelled of smoke and oil, which I later found out were kerosene tanks and candles. Since we were living from place to place for so long, every dealer and addict knew us by name.

My name is Kassandra, but everybody calls me Kassie. I never was a looker growing up, but that didn't matter, because my body was fully developed by age thirteen. Growing up wearing my brother's and my mother's clothes made me rather just be naked. That's when I felt pretty.

My first boyfriend—or man, I should say—was twenty-three years old, and I was fourteen. What started off as business eventually turned into love, I guess. He picked me up one morning walking down Lincoln Way. It was early, and most kids my age would've been heading to school. I was wearing a short skirt and some stilettos, with lipstick and my mama's wig.

"Hey, Kassie," Ricky yelled. He was out at Adam's gas station getting some blunts. He had a Chevy Impala with tinted windows. His car was a pretty red color and matched my shoes, so I decided to let him give me a ride.

"What are you doing out this early, Ricky?" I asked. I knew him because he was one of the dealers who served my mother from time to time.

"I got to get an early start. Early bird gets the first worm," he told me, showing me his bankroll of money.

"That's more money than I ever seen in my life," I told him as a joke, hoping he'd offer me some without me having to throw my legs up.

Ricky was a heavyset, light-skinned guy. He was always dressed nice and kind of cute to me. For some reason, I was attracted to fat guys. I knew he smelled me, because I could smell myself. When I cracked my window to let some fresh air inside the car, he gave me a look but just let it go.

We were smoking a blunt of kush when we were pulled over by the police. I had been wanted by CPS (Child Protective Services) for quite some time at that point, but I still didn't hesitate to take his dope sock and stuff it up in my nasty panties.

"You turned without using a turn signal," the white officer told Ricky.

"I live right up the street; I was almost home. Can't all this wait?"

"What kind of question is that? Show me a valid driver's license and maybe you only get a ticket," the officer said.

"Roll down your window the rest of the way," a female officer in her late twenties asked me through the cracked window. I did, which let out a horrific smell of dead fish, causing her to immediately step back away from the car.

I was embarrassed but also glad. Who cared what she thought about the way I smelled? It was Ricky I was scared to face. He didn't show me any emotions at all.

Once we got to his house, which was nice but inside the hood, he took me upstairs to his bedroom and gave me one of his wifebeaters and a pair of his boxers, which were huge but made me smile. Then he took me back downstairs to the bathroom, ran the water for me in the tub, and handed me a towel. I took off my mama's wig and looked at myself in the mirror. I couldn't help but smile—I looked a hot mess!

By the time I finished washing up, the tub had a dark ring around it from my filthy body. I used my towel and scrubbed it clean, and then I found a new toothbrush in his medicine cabinet. I looked again in the mirror at myself, and I looked worse than before. My hair was all matted up, and my face was broken out from constantly putting on makeup. I tried to wrap my dirty towel around my head in a sexy way before heading back upstairs.

"Can you cook?" Ricky asked me. He was in the kitchen cooking up some crack. He had a box of Arm & Hammer baking soda, a Pyrex container, and a bowl of ice cubes.

"Cook what?" I asked, confused.

"Bacon, eggs, grits, toast," he offered, never taking his eyes off the microwave for a second. He kept opening up the microwave and using a butter knife to stir up the crack. It smelled like burning glue.

"Yeah, I can figure out how to. Why you want me to cook?" I asked.

"I don't care. Are you hungry?"

"Not really. I don't eat breakfast!"

He didn't pay me any more attention. I went and sat on his couch. Before I knew it, I was fast asleep.

CHAPTER 1

It was six in the morning when I finally said to myself *fuck it* and got up off my bunk. Today was my eighteenth birthday, which meant my probation officer had no other choice but to order my release. I had been at the Juvenile Justice Center's residential program for more than two years. It could've been a lot less, but unfortunately I wasn't able to pass the GED test so I could get released early.

"Hey, girl!" Lindsay said to me as she came out of her room. She had a towel in one hand and her toothbrush in the other. She had been at the JJC just as long as me. She had a crush on one of the black boys locked up with us, so she intentionally failed the GED test just so she could stay.

"Hey there, beautiful," I told her with a huge smile on my face. Even though most of us were around the same age, all of the girls looked up to me because they all knew I was a mother and a prostitute at a very young age. One of the program's requirements was to tell our life stories to the group. I was mostly truthful about mine. Even after the group, all of the girls would come to my room and want me to tell them stories about growing up in the ghetto streets.

"Kassandra," Christina yelled. She was a female guard who always gave me a hard time. "Your probation officer sent a pass for you!"

I knew that was for the officer to hand me my walking papers, but for some reason I dreaded seeing her. All of my homegirls were clapping for me and all, but I was sad. I didn't know what was next for me back out in the world. My family was there . . .

As I waited out in front of her office, I was almost in tears. Her name was Cathy Blight. She was young, blonde, maybe twenty-five years old, and she drove the coolest car in the world, a Nissan 3000 Z. I loved her and her car.

1

Cathy was like a mother to me. The whole time I was incarcerated at the facility, she took me to see my son, Carlton, at his foster parents' house. She taught me how to drive and dress like a lady. She would take me to nice restaurants and teach me how to eat properly. It was crazy, but what I feared most about leaving was never seeing her again.

"Hi, Kassie!" Cathy said to me as I entered her office. Her back was to me. She was bent over, looking through files, trying to find the papers for me to sign.

"Hey," I sadly said.

When she turned around and faced me, there were tears in her eyes. I jumped up and reached out to her, and she embraced me. We held each other for a few minutes, and then she said, "So, are you going to check in with me?"

"Yes!" I said without letting her go.

"You're going to get a job?"

"Yes."

She pushed me out to arm's length, still holding me so she could look in my eyes. "Kassie, I am going to miss you like crazy," she said, "but I want you to be strong out there. Now, your brother has a room set up for you at his house. I want you to take your time and not rush into anything."

"I'm scared!"

"You should be, but you're a strong girl. I think you'll be just fine."

After meeting with Cathy, I went back to give all of my things away to my friends. Lindsay and I exchanged information and promised to keep in contact with one another. The staff members and all of the girls threw me a surprise birthday party. They invited the boys from across the hall, too, which wasn't normal—the staff knew the boys tried to sneak feels and stuff on the girls—but with me going home on my birthday, they made an exception to the rules.

My brother made it on time to pick me up. He was the only one of my family members who had visited me while I was locked up. My little sister, Jackie, ended up with foster parents and moved to Florida. She wrote me a few times, but I never wrote back. I think being locked up made me bitter. Word was that she found a good mom and was living out in the country on a farm, but who knows.

"So are you ready to go?" Carlton asked me after eating a slice of my birthday cake. I was also eating cake and drinking punch. Funny how at eighteen years old, I was still enjoying cake and ice cream—maybe because growing up I only remember getting a Dilly bar and a Hostess cake for my party. My mother would use her children's birthday parties as a reason to invite over our useless aunties, just so they could get drunk and high.

"Yeah, bro, I am ready," I said, breaking from my trance.

"Bye, Kassie!" Lindsay said. She was so sweet. Here I was, dark-skinned, petite, and from the streets. She was blonde, with very nice body, and from the suburbs. Somehow we became best friends. "I will call you when I go on my next pass."

"That's fine! Call my brother's number. Be good and get your butt out of here . . ."

"Okay!" Lindsay said under her breath with a pout. She always did that whenever I told her something everybody else was telling her as well. We were connected that way.

Once my brother and I finally left the building, everything changed. When I got out to the car, I saw there were already two of his homeboys sitting in the car with blunts rolled up and bottles of Bebicka vodka in the backseat waiting for me. First thing I did was kick the back of my brother's seat after I got in behind him.

"Boy, you going to get me back locked up on my first day home," I told my brother.

"Girl, chill out. You been gone for two years. I know you need a drink."

"You right, bro," I said before taking the bottle from Jeff, who was sitting next to me in the back. Then I looked over at him and realized he was a boy I had a crush on growing up but knew was too cute to take me seriously. But now I had a perm, my hair done up in a wrap. Cathy had taken me to get my nails done up in a French manicure style with her. She would always take me and Lindsay along; the two of them would get tanned up, and I always got nails and a new perm. It was crazy, because I got my first perm while locked up, so not only did I learn how to put it in perfectly by myself, I also did all of the other girls' hair for them, white and black.

I looked at myself in the mirror from the backseat, and for the first time in my life I saw myself and felt like I was beautiful. My hair was banging. I had on a skull cap with a brim on it, a North Face jacket to match, and some lip gloss that made my lips look luscious and good. I'd known I needed to check myself out from the way my brother's friends were barking at me when I walked up to the car.

"You want to go see Mama?" Bro asked me, also looking at himself in the mirror and making eye contact with me. We were so much alike, which was weird because we had different daddies, yet we were identical almost.

"Not now! She didn't come see me the whole time I was in there."

"I know, but she's still your mother," he told me protectively. "Besides, I need to go over there to bust a serve anyway."

"Bust a serve?" I asked, all too familiar with that term from the year or so I spent living from trap house to trap house with Ricky.

"You heard me!"

"I know you ain't selling that shit now, Bro?" I asked.

He never answered me. He knew I lost my baby's father to that shit. I thought to myself, silent and distant, about that night. I lost my freedom, and Ricky lost his life, and our son lost us both. A tear came into the corner of my eye, but I shook it off. Instead, I grabbed the blunt from Jeff and took a hit that caused me to choke up a storm.

As much as I wanted to relive that past nightmare in my mind, I could not. I was free, with a new look and a new way of looking at life. I loved Ricky and always would miss him, but I could be laying next to him in that funeral home. What he did was stupid.

CHAPTER 2

"Hey, baby! You look so nice!" my mother yelled at me as soon as I came in the door. She was looking like she'd aged twenty years since I last saw her.

"Hey, Mama," I said before giving her a hug. She kissed me on the cheek, which was a familiar feeling.

"You hungry? Girl, how you been? How's that baby?" she kept going at a hundred miles a second.

"Carlton," I corrected her.

"Oh, yeah, Carlton," she said apologetically. "After your brother?"

"Yeah. You talked to Jackie?"

"No! She is gone to college or something . . ."

"You don't know?" I asked, offended.

Before she could answer me, Carlton came running up from the basement. He looked at me and asked, "You ready?"

"Yeah!"

We left and promised to come back over later. I could say that she was doing better than the last time I saw her. She had a boyfriend who was taking care of her, so she wasn't living on the streets.

After my brother took me to Linden Grill, we went over to the studio that was next to Frankie's BBQ. The moment we got out of the car, the smell of the ribs and special barbecue sauce hit my nose. I wanted to get some ribs as well, but I decided to save my money. Cathy had given me twenty dollars before I left, which wasn't going to last long if I went in Frankie's.

Once we got into the studio, there were people everywhere. Marcos, the driver, took it upon himself to introduce me to everybody like I was his date. He even told one of his friends I was going to be his li'l boo, which I thought was sexy because it had been a long time since any man called me *boo*, and it seemed like a lifetime since I had some dick. I let him know that, too, but through body language.

Marcos was cute. He had a swagger about him that turned me on. He was tall, skinny, and dressed like he had money. His car was nice too; it was a girly car, but it had tints and a nice stereo inside and would look good if I was driving it.

"How old are you?" I asked him after we were finally done greeting everybody. He was sitting next to me on the couch. Everybody else was busy writing raps to the beats that were playing so loud I had to yell for him to hear me.

"Twenty-two. Why?"

"I just wondered, that's all."

"Want to go out to the car so we can talk without yelling?" he asked me. I knew it was an invite, and he knew that's exactly what I was waiting for.

"That's cool . . ." I said while giving my brother the eye. He looked at me and then shrugged his shoulders. Even though he was a year older than me, he looked at me like I was the oldest. Maybe it's because there was a time when I made money to feed us all. Seemed so long ago, but it was still reality.

When we got out to the car and I got in the front seat, it felt weird. Last time I was in a car with a man, it was Ricky. I was Ricky's personal assistant; he always made me drive him around and even drive myself around to go handle his business for him. I didn't even know how to drive at first, but after a few bumps and fender benders, I got good at it.

Marcos was texting the whole time. He didn't say one word to me. I was confused, because I wanted him to make the first move. He had no clue that all he had to do was touch me or even hint at it, and I would've fucked him right then and there.

"You feel like riding with me somewhere?" he asked, but he sounded frustrated, like he had an attitude.

"Where?"

"Man, my cousin needs me to drive somewhere for him."

"You going to bust a serve?" I asked, already sick and tired of dope deals within the first couple hours home. All the time I spent locked up for drug charges—for drugs that weren't even mine—made me hate that shit.

"I don't sell dope," he replied, taking off as if I'd agreed to go with him.

"What do you do?" I curiously asked. I was rolling up the blunt he handed me soon as we got in the car and having a rough time getting the blunt to stick.

"I'm a driver!" he told me, driving and texting at the same time.

"A getaway driver," I joked, firing up the blunt at the same time, holding it so it would stick together, passing it to him.

"My cousin pays me to drive him and his girls around."

At first when he told me this, I just let it go into one ear and out the other. Who cared what he did and who he worked for? My mind was on something else. All the weed and liquor were running through my body, so I wanted to relax and, honestly, get fucked really hard.

We pulled up to a townhouse of some sort out in Georgetown by Notre Dame. There were cars lined up on the side of the house in the grass. There was a Cadillac, a big black van, and a black SUV. The front door was open, and from the looks of it, there was a party going on.

Marcos was still texting somebody on the phone. I had no idea what he was doing, but as soon as we walked into the house, I was greeted at the door by Marcos's cousin. He was tall, had his shirt off, and was exposing his tattoos and beer belly. He was wearing some Jordan basketball shorts and sandals and had a blunt in his mouth. He grabbed my hand and kissed it.

"Heard a lot about you," he told me, causing me to immediately look over my shoulder at Marcos.

"What did you hear about me?" I asked, confused. There were maybe five or six women running around getting dressed. I didn't know why, but I felt like I was out of place. They were all beautiful in different ways: thick, white, skinny, black . . .

"I heard you were fine, with a banging body," he told me, still holding my hand at a distance to have a look.

"You did?"

"Yes, and I heard you just got out of jail today and need to find a job."

"I never told him that," I snapped.

"Look," he told me, showing me his iPhone screen with a picture of me walking out of JJC saved on it. "Isn't that you?"

"Yeah, but how did you get that?"

"Long story! Look, do you want to go with us?"

"Where ya'll going?" I asked, scared but interested at the same time. There was something about this guy that was powerful. It was an energy I'd never been around before. He wasn't asking me, he was telling me.

"Chicago!"

"Chicago?"

"Yeah, but don't worry. We coming back in the morning. We only going to go until six a.m. and then coming back. Cool?"

I didn't answer. He wasn't asking me anyway. Marcos couldn't look me in the eye either. He'd set me up. It was all making sense. His cousin was a pimp.

Here I was, a retired prostitute, and on my first day out of jail I get introduced to a pimp. I never had a pimp before. I had watched movies, I had read books about them, but I never thought I would meet one. He never told me he was one either. Soon as I realized I was on my way to Chicago, I had a seat. My mother, Cathy, my brother, my son, all went through my mind for a brief second. I knew I still had a choice, but deep down inside, I also felt at home. It was crazy, too, because for the first time in my life I actually knew what I was about to get myself into. I was scared, and it felt good.

None of the girls said anything to me. It was just like being looked up, because before anyone says anything to you, they size you up. At first you pose a threat, but then you become an associate. A simple nod is all it takes. I sat there silent. I watched everything, but I paid extra attention to the pimp. He moved around the room so fluidly. It was like he was with every one of the girls. I watched him help one girl who was taking pictures of another girl with his phone. Then he sat next to me and helped another girl put an address into a GPS, and then he went into the bathroom where another girl was using a curling iron to fix her hair. He was everywhere—I got confused just watching him.

"Papa!" I heard someone yell from upstairs. She was loud, and as soon as she yelled for him, he went running up the stairs. I couldn't see or hear anything, but I wondered how many girls were up there and what they looked like. So far, it was pretty even. There were three black girls and two white girls, and from the sound of her voice, this other girl sounded white.

I sat for a few seconds alone on the couch while everybody ignored me. Marcos wasn't anywhere to be found either. It was like nobody cared who I was; they passed me the blunts that seemed to come from every direction. I almost fell asleep sitting there.

"Kassandra!" I heard the pimp yell from upstairs. It startled me. "Come up here!"

"Okay," I yelled back, adrenaline rushing through my body. I went up not quite knowing what to expect.

There were three doors at the top of the stairs, all closed. I heard yelling or arguing behind one, with loud music playing. It sounded like Mariah Carey, but a song I had never heard before, and it was jamming. Sitting there waiting for something to happen, I started dancing. Crazy part is that growing up living with my mother, dancing was the only way I could take myself from the reality of what was going on around me. This was like that same feeling all over again.

"Hi!" This girl scared me as she opened up the master bedroom door. "I'm going to be putting you under my wing tonight, so come on inside," she said.

"Putting me under your wing?"

Ignoring my question, she said, "You're a petite little thing, aren't you?"

Embarrassed, I said, "Yes."

"Well, let me see. I may have some heels for you and some leggings. Then you will need some makeup. I don't know if you can fit into any of my dresses." She kept talking to herself as if I wasn't there or as if she was fitting me up for a dress. "Take your clothes off!"

"All of them?"

"Yes, I need to see the goods."

"Where is he?" I whispered, referring to the pimp.

"Who, Papa Bear?" she giggled. "Girl, he see plenty pussy all day every day. Trust and believe he going to test these waters soon enough."

"What?"

"Girl, relax! I am just saying, the nigga good at what he do, and he like petite little fine honeys like yourself. Damn, girl, look at these titties! Them have to be the nicest set I've ever seen," she said, turning me to face the mirror on top of the dresser.

"Thank you!"

"Papa!" she yelled to him. I could see his new white socks, boxers, and V-neck T-shirt sitting on the edge of the king-size bed. It was the largest bed I'd ever seen. From the looks of things, I could tell that he was in the shower. I sat there and waited in the mirror for him with my shirt off, looking at myself. I'd grown up over the years. Those aluminum mirrors in our cells back at JJC never did justice to my figure. This was the first time in years I had seen my full body in the mirror. My belly was tight and firm from working out regularly; my ass looked firm and good. I was a lady.

I saw her looking at me in the mirror, kind of sizing me up but not in a jealous way—fitting me for clothes. She was beautiful, by far the prettiest girl in the house. She had blonde highlights in her hair, her body was athletic, nice round ass, with some tiger paws on her right cheek. Her waist was slim, her chest small but average, and her skin looked very tanned up. She was a bad bitch.

"What's up?" Papa Bear yelled, coming in the room in nothing but a towel. He didn't even look at me, as if I wasn't standing there half naked.

"Look at these boobs on this hot mama here!" she told him, grabbing my arms down from over my chest.

"Nice," he said. "She needs to get rid of them grandma panties though and shave."

Embarrassed, I asked, "Excuse me?"

"Stacey will get you some thongs."

"I've never worn thongs before!"

Without even considering my request to not change my panties, Stacey was in her top drawer getting a handful of brand-new panties from Victoria's Secret for me to choose from. They were all nice—pinks, blues, white, and the color I picked, black.

"Look, Papa," Stacey told him, proud. "Girl, that's our color. Look at my nails. We all wear black tips on our nails and black or dark colors when we working the track."

"It's been years since I've been on the track." I laughed under my breath. They both looked at me at the same time.

"How old are you?" Papa asked me.

"Eighteen today!"

"Today is your birthday?"

"Yeah!"

"I will take you someplace nice when we get to Chicago to celebrate."

The rest of the time we spent at the house, I was getting all dolled up. It was actually fun, because it had been years since I put makeup on, and the girl had about a million dollars' worth of shit everywhere. I was sober by the time we got done. She made me shave my pussy bald, which was itchy at first, but cute. She put me in some brand-new black leggings, a black top, some black heels, and her down jacket. I looked just like a classy grown woman. I loved it!

When I came down the stairs, everybody was gone. Only people left were Marcos and Papa Bear. They was both eyeballing me as I came down the stairs.

"Damn!" Marcos yelled. His mouth dropped open.

"You look nice," Papa Bear said.

I walked up, and they were both standing there like they were waiting to see who I was ready to share my beauty, my body, my loyalty with.

"Thank you, Papa!" I said and then stood next to him while rolling my eyes at Marcos. I knew it would hurt his feelings, but he set me up. How could he expect me to just jump into his arms?

"I'm ready!" Stacey said, finally coming down the stairs. "They all on the road already?"

"You already know they better beat me there instead of meet me there!" Papa joked in his pimp slang.

"I don't care if them hos was there for two hours before us, they won't even make half of what I make on my first date."

"You sure about that?"

"Papa, don't play with me. You know you got the baddest bitch in the game. I taught them bitches everything they know! I know what they capable of."

I was just absorbing everything. Marcos stormed out to the car first. I followed him. The car was nice. It was a baby-blue Cadillac with a white leather top, white leather seats, and a set of chrome rims with tires and a chrome grill on the front. It looked expensive. I sat up front next to Marcos. He didn't speak to me, and I didn't speak to him. Hell, I didn't know him any better than Mama and Papa Bear. What did he expect? He should've fucked me when he had the chance. Now he would never see this pussy!

CHAPTER 3

Chicago was everything I expected it to be. Other than the slow-moving traffic that filled the streets, it was beautiful. I had never been outside of South Bend, Indiana, so coming to the city was like a dream come true.

One of the girls I had been locked up with was from Chicago, so I was scared at first from all the horror stories she told us in group from her childhood, but it seemed like something out of a movie to me. There weren't any gangs or thugs running around with guns and their pants sagging. It was all white college students and businessmen wearing suits and ties.

Mama was on the phone nonstop the whole ride up to Chicago. It was like once Papa Bear posted an ad for us off his iPhone, her phone just kept ringing. I was getting confused. She talked the same way to everybody. She talked with a pen in her hand and wrote down address after address.

I sat back and soaked up as much game as I could, which was an awful lot. She wasn't actually teaching me how to cover the calls or explaining to me what we were going to have to do. She just kept telling me that I would be able to cover calls just like her and that it was all about sticking to the script.

"Papa," she said sadly, "my regular on Dearborn wants me to stop by for an hour."

"Okay . . ." he said sarcastically. He was busy working his phone and was just as busy as she was on her phone, except he was posting ads and checking e-mails.

"You going to make me go?"

"Of course!"

"But I hate seeing this weird fuck. All he wants is for me to pee all in his mouth, and his apartment is so sickening. Cats all over the place. I hate seeing him. I got all these other addresses for both of us, and he only got two hundred dollars."

"Sounds like a date to me," he told her without looking up from his phone. "Marcos, do you know the way?"

"Yeah, I got it. It's off Division and Dearborn. I will park in the Jewel/Osco parking lot, cool?"

"I don't like walking over there. Can't you drop me off closer?" she asked him, but really she was asking Papa.

Without any notice, Papa slapped her across her face. It was so fast that I couldn't even see anything, but I heard it, and it sounded like it hurt. It sent a chill through my body.

When we finally parked, Mama was out the car before we could come to a complete stop. She slammed the door so hard that the car shook even after she was out of sight.

I looked at her in her black dress and heels and realized why she wanted to be dropped closer—because unlike the more posh, upscale downtown area we went through coming off of the highway, there were homeless people and drug addicts everywhere. I was scared for her.

He must of noticed my fear, because he said, "Come on . . . I want you to take a walk with me."

"Where?" I asked, but again, he wasn't asking me, he was telling me to join him. I did.

We walked up Division toward State Street, which made me feel a little better. There was a massive crowd of people partying, but also Chicago police SUVs and cars lined up along the side of the street. We walked past hundreds of bars within one block. There were pizza parlors that sold Chicago-style pizza by the slice, and there were Greek spots that sold gyros along with burgers and Chicago-style hotdogs, but we avoided all of those grease spots and went into this nice Mexican sports bar off the corner of State Street with outdoor seating.

There were at least five hundred people inside the restaurant. I could barely keep up with him as he pulled me behind him through the crowd. I was so small compared to everybody else . . . or maybe I just felt small.

Once we got to the back, there was a table waiting for us. There was a sign with *Reserved* written on it. Papa took the sign, handed it off to a waitress who winked at him, and then we had a seat. I was impressed.

"So, how is everything so far?" he asked me without taking his eyes off of his phone. He was back to work.

"I don't know . . ." I hesitated. This man was a monster with a cute smile and a swagger that I'd never seen. I hadn't ever been slapped by a man before, and although I hoped I never would be, I wished it would've been me instead of Mama.

He looked up at me with those same threatening eyes, but he didn't speak until the waitress finished placing our Top Shelf Margaritas in front of us with the extra shot of Patrón on the side, some lemon wedges, and again, a wink. "You don't know what?" he continued after first smashing his shot.

I sipped my drink. "I don't know what the hell to think," I snapped, showing that I wasn't scared of him at all. Actually, I was turned on by all this, but I knew better than to let him know that.

"That's good. You see, I am going to teach you how to think, and don't worry, it's simple," he smiled. I could hear the liquor in his voice. "You will learn the main rules today. Then the rest will come naturally as long as you put these rules top-priority."

"I'm listening," I snapped again, realizing he liked it the first time.

"Okay. You have to be deaf, dumb, and blind—"

"Excuse me?" I asked, but in a swift motion his hand was over my mouth to shut me up. He didn't realize it, but him putting his hand over my mouth sent a electric shock wave from my lips down into my freshly shaved pussy. It was right then and there that I knew I had to have him inside me.

"Being deaf means, no matter what you hear, you act like you didn't hear it, and I don't care if a trick calls you a nigger bitch, you act like you like to be called a nigger bitch. Being dumb means that you are not even smart enough to know what you heard even if you did hear it, and being blind means that even if you see a badge on a trick's wallet you are too blind to see it, too dumb to understand it, and too deaf to hear," he explained without taking a breath.

"Got it!" I playfully told him while giving him eye contact. He had the most mischievous eyes I'd ever seen. They were dark and deep. They held pain . . .

For a minute, I expected him to kiss me, but that shit only happens in the movies. Instead of a nice romantic kiss, he picked up his drink and offered me a toast.

"Till death do us part," he joked, but despite the wicked smile on his face, I knew he was very serious. I hesitated before I clinked my glass against his.

"Till death do us part," I said.

"Okay, you are now married to the game," he yelled, but only loud enough for me to hear him.

"And what exactly does that mean?"

"It means you are going to be a boss bitch. It means that you will learn the tricks and trades of the game. It means that you will make more money than you ever dreamed."

"Sounds nice, but what do I get in the end?" I asked, curious as to what he was getting at but afraid to ask.

He looked at me but never answered my question. We finished our drinks and then left to meet Marcos and Mama out front. Mama was in the backseat smiling at me, but as soon as Papa Bear got inside the car, she frowned at him.

It was weird to me too, because I could see the Mommy and Daddy roles they played. She was just like a mother. She made sure that I felt welcome and at home with them. I could see how she was the leader or "bottom bitch." None of the other girls made me feel as comfortable as she did, and none of the other girls stood up to Papa the way she did. They all had like this fake smile or phony giggle, but as soon as he walked away or left the room, they either rolled their eyes or smacked their lips. Mama was open about her feelings.

"Did you have a drink?" she asked me, catching me off guard.

"Yeah girl, and it was the bomb!" I giggled. It really was delicious.

"Good! Well, I hope you're ready to get down to business, because we have a date down at West Michigan Avenue."

"Okay, I'm ready!" I said, and I was. I knew I could do dates. I grew up knowing that I could do dates.

"Papa!" she sarcastically said, "this bitch is going to be a pro before you know it."

"I told you she had it naturally," he agreed, still focused on his phone. "Did you check on this hotel date? You know I hate hotels, Mama."

"Yes, Papa," she mockingly murmured. "He is in town on business. He has an out-of-state number from Tennessee. I checked the number, it's legit. He said he was married and very generous."

"What's wrong with hotels?" I asked now, a little nervous. They were talking about things that I never would've been worried about, but I needed to know what to expect.

"You see, there are different cities that you have to work different. Big cities like Chicago or anywhere that has a large police force usually have a special force designated to busting us bitches. They set up in hotels and call us out to them and then bust us for prostitution. That's why we come here, because it is that much easier for them to just bust you at the hotel than have you go to them," she explained while reapplying her makeup.

"So, what's it called if we sit in rooms?"

"That's called doing-in calls, which mostly you want to do in college towns or anywhere in the South. I do both anywhere, but that's after I take extra precautions. It's all about the script. The script helps you to get a feel of what the trick is on and if he is playing or serious. True dates will respect the script and know that you know what you're doing on the phone. It is just as easy to tell if you know what you're doing as it is to be able to tell if they are real."

"I don't understand," I admitted.

She held her little notebook up to me. There were at least twenty addresses written down. "These are not all real, but the ones that I feel are real I put first. In a big city like this, there is a lot of competition: other pimps, escort services, and renegade hos. They call and try to send the competition to fake dates so that we get too far away and then once the dates that are good get tired of waiting for us, they call them. They get the leftovers."

"That's dirty!" I managed to say.

"Yeah, but I don't worry about the competition because when I hit a city I come in so heavy that no matter where a trick looks for a date, he will end up calling one of my bitches," Papa said cockily. "It's expensive, too, because these postings are not free, and I am running ten dollar ads per hour on any one site at a time, which means I could easily spend five hundred on just gas and posting in a night."

"Damn," was all I could say.

"That's why we play team ball. I send the other bitches to the dates that are far away, they send dates to me as well as the others, and we always, always let each car know about fake addresses or possible police setups," Mama said before covering another call.

I sat back and listened to her for the first time, trying to understand the script, but I couldn't see anything special at all. It seemed basic. However, I stayed quiet. It was one of the top-priority rules to play dumb, so I did. Deep down inside, I knew I could answer the phone.

"I am parking at the King Burrito on St. Clair and Ohio," Marcos said. "They can catch the cab from there, because I am not about to pull up to the hotel in this caddy." He was trying to make me nervous, I could tell.

"That's cool. I need to reload my Green Dot anyway. I can go to the 7-Eleven on the corner."

"I'm glad the driver is making up his own rules!" Mama snapped loudly and sarcastically. She knew she was right, too. For a minute, I thought Papa was going to slap her again, but he just stayed focused on his phone.

We parked on the corner, and before we could complain any more, we were out of the car. There were cabs everywhere, but instead of jumping in the first one, we went to Dunkin' Donuts. I had drunk too much already to be able to eat a donut, although they looked good, so I got a medium coffee with cream and sugar. To my surprise, the mixture was perfect. They made the best cup of coffee I had ever tasted.

"Look, Kassandra," Mama said, getting my attention. I could tell she was about to tell me something important that I needed to hear. "When we get there, I want you to follow my lead."

She went on, "There are so many girls out there who think what we do is all about fucking for money, but there is much more to it than that. What sets all of us apart from professional to elite status is having the ability to make these clients feel the experience of a lifetime. Most of these guys are married, so they have a wife at home to lay down and fuck, but they can't fulfill their fantasies at home with their wives. They want the ultimate experience of being catered to by a hot chick. They want to be able to feel like they are in a dream. They don't want to be fucked, they want to be pleased in any and every way possible. And guess what?"

"What?" I asked, interested and in a way understanding.

"They are willing to pay for that experience of a lifetime. It's priceless."

I wanted to jump in and explain to her that I gave the best head in the world, or that my pussy was the wettest, warmest place on Earth, but the truth was, I knew that was a lie. This was time for me to listen. It was time to be deaf.

To tell the truth, I was nervous. I felt my stomach turn so fast that I could've thrown up. It felt like the feeling before you get on a roller-coaster ride, kind of knowing it's going to go fast and in every direction possible, and that it is a dangerous but exciting ride. I was so scared walking through the lavish lobby of the hotel that I reached out like an innocent child would reach out to her mother if she was scared. Funny thing was, everybody gave us the dirtiest looks I'd ever received in my life. The women turned up their noses and the men licked their lips, but we had a date to go to, which was on the top floor of the nicest hotel I'd ever been in.

Waiting for the door to open up was the longest I'd waited for anything, it seemed, even though it only took a moment. Once it swung open and I saw who was waiting on us, I almost melted. It was the sexiest man I'd ever seen.

"Hi there! You are one hot lady," he said to Mama. "What should I call you?"

"Shirley Temple!" she exclaimed. "This is my girlfriend, Kassie."

"Kassie, huh?" he asked me, now taking my hand in his. He was so charming, and more romantic than I had ever experienced. "So, are you girls willing to entertain each other as well as me?"

"Sure," I said. I was excited for some reason—maybe because I still hadn't gotten any sex since my release, which seemed like an eternity ago. Life was moving so fast for me.

"Let's not jump straight into all the questions. First things first. I have a contract here in my possession for you to sign with some form of identification that states who you are, that you are not any form of the law, and that anything that happens here tonight is between us as consenting adults," Mama said, catching me and him off guard.

"There is no need for all of that," he explained. "I am not trying to do anything but get laid by two lovely ladies tonight. I don't want any trouble."

"Us either!" she stated with the typed-up contract in her hand now. "However, this is business."

I sat back and watched in amazement as they went back and forth. Mama was not budging, and he wasn't either. I decided to go to the restroom to relieve myself. There was nothing I could say to convince either of them what to do.

The restroom was nice, too, but the first thing that caught my attention was that it looked as if it had not been used. The toilet-paper roll was still brand new and folded into a triangle, and the towels were all neatly folded. It was too perfect, like it wasn't supposed to be touched.

As I sat down to use the toilet, I heard a noise that sent shivers up my spine. There was another voice speaking in the room. It was another female voice, and it wasn't friendly.

The pounding on the bathroom door made my heart shake. "Hey, you in there, open up the door and come out with both hands up!" the female voice said sternly.

"Here I come!"

"Hurry, and don't flush that toilet," she demanded.

I flushed anyway. "Okay!"

"Get your little ass out here!" she yelled, pounding again.

I opened the door, and they were all standing around looking at me. There were three of them: one heavyset black cop with a suit on, a white lady officer, very pretty, and a Hispanic guy who seemed to be in charge. Mama sat at the end of the bed and did not look scared one bit.

"Don't say shit to them!" Mama said to me, confident. "They don't got shit on us."

"You know what, she's right," the sexy guy who set us up said as he walked into the room again with the contract in his hand and a badge around his neck. "We don't have shit on you two, which actually, I like you both. You two are the most professional of the night. However, you're still going to jail. It may not stick, but you're going to be charged. As long as we can get as many of you prostitutes off the streets as we can for the night, we can save as many happy homes, hard-earned money, and honest people as we can. That's our job."

"Some job! Think of how much money you waste on all this!" Mama yelled. "You might as well let us go."

"Well, actually, it costs us nothing. We have more girls next door. We got all of them for prostitution charges and took their money and phones, which will give us information on the tricks and possible pimps," the pretty female officer said, emphasizing the word *pimp*, like she hated them the most. Or maybe like she had a secret admiration for them; I could sense something.

"What are we going to jail for then?" I asked, confused.

"Trespassing!" the sexy cop said after handing me my phone and identification back. "You just got out today, I see."

"Kind of sort of," I smiled, still turned on by him. "It's after midnight, so yesterday."

"Well, guess what?" he said, handing me his card. "Today is your lucky day. I'm willing to let you go, as long as you promise to use this."

I looked at his card and then flipped it over to see that it read, *My personal cell, you're cute! Hope you call me,* with a smiley face on it. My heart skipped a beat. Was he serious? I wasn't *that* gullible.

"As long as you let us both go!" I demanded, looking him up and down with a smile on.

"Wait a minute!" the pretty female officer said. "You can't let them go!"

"You listen to me, I'm in charge here, and I can do as I please. If I was you, I would learn my position and the proper way to address your superior," he pointed out while walking up face to face. "Now, I said, I am letting them go. They're legit. Get over it."

She looked at me and stuck her nose up. That's when I realized she was one of the people in the lobby who put her nose up at us as we walked in. She left and slammed the door so loud that I jumped.

The man handed Mama the contract that saved our asses, and then he led us to the door. There was just a vibe he gave me that made me melt. He was amazing.

"I promise to use it," I whispered in his ear, "but you have to come to Indiana to see me. I am cool on Chicago."

"I would love to," he whispered back. "Now be careful. Don't want to see you again tonight."

"Thank you!" Mama told him.

"Don't thank me. Thank your friend Kassandra here."

CHAPTER 4

I woke up with a hangover the next morning. Marcos and I slept together on an air mattress upstairs in the spare bedroom, but I didn't have sex with him. I was sore from the date that I did do in Chicago with a black guy from the South Side Wild 100s.

The bastard was supposed to give me a hundred dollars, but he only had seventy. Then he fucked my brains out for so long and hard I thought I was a virgin, I bled so much. It was horrible. He was stinky, like he hadn't taken a shower in a month. His breath stunk like copper from his gold teeth, and oh my, he was huge! I mean *huge*! He was cute, though, in a way. Kind of like maybe I could've cleaned his ass up and made a good man out of him. He had huge muscles like he had done time in prison and had a full body of tattoos. I will never forget him!

"You hungry?" Mama asked me as soon as I got downstairs. She was standing in the kitchen wearing Daddy's robe and cleaning up behind him as he cooked. He was making pancakes and bacon, and boy was the food looking good.

"Yeah, sure," I said, mouth watering. This was the best food I'd seen in all the time that I spent locked up. "You still up?"

"Please! I don't sleep without my Papa," she said all excited, like last night never happened.

I looked around the living room, and there were people laid out everywhere. One on the couch, two on the floor, and even one in the bathroom, cleaning up and getting ready to run to a date. They had all come from Chicago, but when we got back, nobody was here. On the table was a big pile of money. There were thousands of dollars spread out. I knew that because just looking at the money, I could see that most of the bills were hundreds.

"How are you doing?" Papa asked me, noticing my eyes.

21

"Oh, good!"

"We got a double date set up this morning," Mama said. "He is a regular of mine, so don't worry, it won't be any surprises."

"Speaking of which," Papa said, "give her her gift."

"Oh," Mama said, and then she reached into the pocket of her robe and handed me an iPhone.

Speechless with my mouth open, I said, "Is this mine?"

"Of course!" Papa interjected. "But it's a business line, not for pleasure."

I couldn't help the smile that formed on my face. "Oh, thank you!"

"Don't thank me, you earned it."

"Shit, not only making seventy dollars," I griped.

"It's not about how much money you made. Money will come. It's about not hesitating when your number was called. It's about how you was a team player, and when you and Mama got caught you was willing to go down with her before getting let go without her. That's what I like, that's what makes a good bitch. Sacrificing for the sake of the team. Then, when you did get a date, even though it was for seventy dollars, you gave me all of it. That's all true team-oriented play. I respect that," he said while trying to flip over a pancake the size of the griddle. "It was nothing for you to go on another date after you got caught up by the police. That showed me you got heart. Not to mention this guy been texting the phone like crazy ever since you left him. Whatever you did to him, he hooked! The man call and texted all night long and all morning. I think you got your first regular!"

"I am straight on him. That dude's dick is so big, I will be lucky to not still be bleeding. That mothafucka was huge!"

"Girl, don't worry, there will be enough little dicks that you will be praying for a big one again. It's just your first time," this white girl named Monica said. She had been there before we left, but this was the first time she spoke to me.

"Good," I smiled. She smiled back, but it wasn't really sincere. She went into the bathroom that was connected to the kitchen and slammed the door hard as hell. I jumped.

"Bitch, you better not be slamming no doors up in here! Have you lost your mind?" Mama yelled. "Matter of fact, you can get the fuck out!"

"I ain't going no fucking where! Give me my 40 percent and I will get out, but I fucked eight tricks last night and didn't get shit! How the fuck this new bitch deserve a gift?" she snapped with her hands on her hips, halfway standing out the bathroom door.

Mama jumped straight on top of her. Monica was at least six feet tall and outweighed Mama by twenty pounds, but that didn't stop Mama. She had Monica in headlock, screaming at her. I could tell Monica knew better than to even try to fight back. She just let Mama get the best of her.

"Chill out!" Papa said after handing me the spatula to watch the food with. Then he broke them apart.

"Tell that crackhead bitch to chill out!" Monica said, but she couldn't even get the words out of her mouth good. Papa slapped her so hard she fell instantly to her knees.

"Bitch! What did you say?"

"Nothing! I didn't mean to."

"Not about her, but about 40 percent?" he asked her with a chilling voice, almost at a mumble.

"Daddy, I am sorry!" she cried, blood running down the side of her face. "I am sorry!"

"Get out!" he told her.

"Papa, it's cool," Mama begged. It was like she was feeling sorry for Monica now all of a sudden.

Papa looked at Mama, and to me, and then to Monica. "I tell you what! All you bitches get the fuck out!"

My heart dropped! I was so scared I didn't know what to do. My legs were shaking, and my palms were sweating. On the way out the front door, I noticed all the girls who had been asleep were now outside smoking cigarettes. They all rolled their eyes at me. It seemed like it was all my fault, but it wasn't.

"Girl, chill out," a black girl named Story said to me, noticing the tears forming in my eyes. She handed me her Newport. I took a drag from it and handed it back. "He be tripping over them pink-toes!"

"Excuse me?" I asked, noticing how strapped she was. She had an amazing body: legs like a baby elephant, hips like a whale, and tits like a pair of watermelons.

"He be tripping over them white bitches. Stay away from them hos."

Her advice was mean, but it made sense, so I tried to see things from her point of view. "What we got to do now?"

"Nothing! He gon' forget he put us out in about ten minutes, then his crazy ass going to come out here like he never even went off in the first place."

"But he never put you out," I tried to figure.

"No, when he talk to one, he talk to all of us. He crazy for real."

"What was wrong with her?" I asked under my breath, looking at Monica.

"That psycho bitch is dick sick, that's all. That bitch crazy as hell too! She want Daddy dick!"

"Dick sick?" I asked with one eyebrow up.

"You know what I mean! The bitch went hard last night. I was in the car with her. She did make a lot of money. Usually, whoever do the most money gets to spent the whole day with Daddy. He takes them shopping, out to eat, nails, and hair, the whole nine. Then takes them to a nice room and fuck they brains out."

"They?" I asked, wondering why she spoke about them instead of herself.

"Well, the pink-toes always make the most around here, so when we run routes, they be in direct competition. Mama usually wins, too, but Monica be right there neck to neck with her. Then there is Liz."

"Which one is Liz?" I wondered, looking around.

"She is Daddy's little princess. She wasn't there last night, but if she would have been, she always outdo Monica. Liz has a man, too, and her man knows she has a pimp. You will see her, trust and believe. When she comes around, Daddy don't pay anybody else any attention."

"What about Mama?"

"She don't give a fuck! She always gone on a date, or she be out partying. They treat Liz like a baby girl. She the only one with a life outside of this."

"Have you ever fucked Daddy?"

"Once."

"How long you been with him?"

"About a year now."

"Once!" I yelled.

"Yeah, but let me make myself clear, it was the best sex I ever experienced in my life. Not just the sex. The whole experience. He treated me like a queen. I will never forget it. I love that man."

After she finished, I got up and walked away. Maybe I was the one tripping, but Story seemed the hater of the crew, a snake in the grass. The way she talked about Daddy made my heart race. The feeling was weird, but I didn't like it, so I avoided her.

Mama was still in the house. There was a commotion inside and a sound like breaking glass; however, nobody else paid attention, so I tried not to either. My adrenaline was pumping, and I didn't know why. I felt out of place for the first time. I sat on the porch, alone for a second, until Story saw it as an opening to get further under my skin. She sat next to me and lit up another square. I was sick of her.

"I really don't know why I got involved with this shit," I lied.

"It's really not that bad," she told me. "I get 40 percent sometimes and take it to my mother. She knows what I do."

"Your mother knows?"

"Hell, yeah. I tell my mother everything. As long as I bring her some cigarettes, she happy, but she is like my only friend now. I came here with a friend, but she left him last time we was down in Florida for another pimp. She caught a bus to go back down there with him after we made it up to Atlantic City. She stupid as hell!"

"Florida, Atlantic City? Where all have you been?" I sat up, at full attention now. Story was now showing me another side of the game. She was not weak like I thought. This bitch had game.

"Girl, just watch! We go everywhere at the drop of a dime. We suppose to be going back to Atlantic City. We go to Jersey a lot because out there them Indian tricks love us black bitches. We always outdo them pink-toes on the track. They need us out there. We protect them from other hos and pimps." She smiled and then tossed her square out into the yard. Monica walked up and picked it up like it was her house and put it in the ashtray from the car, which she held in her hand.

"What y'all talking about?" Monica asked after first squeezing in between us on the porch. I think she was trying to make a point, because her left cheek, where I sat, was swollen up and her lip was still bleeding. She was showing off her battle wounds like it was some form of affection. If I wouldn't have known any better, I would say she was in a good mood.

"Excuse you!" Story said sarcastically. There was love between them, almost sisterly. It was weird, because even though they seemed to dislike each other, there was still love. I was confused. "I am telling her about Jersey."

"You coming with us?"

"I . . . I guess so?"

"Girl, Jersey is the shit. The mall out in Elizabeth is my favorite mall in the world. I get all my dresses from there. The clothes are all nice and cheap without tax." Monica was excited. "Oh, you know, when we go to Jersey, we always spend a couple days in Pittsburgh on the way too."

"I hate Pittsburgh," Story said. "It's pretty, but it's too big and slow, with some scary-ass hills. The money is good, but it's hard work."

"And hot, too! The police, he on some straight-up bullshit."

"When we suppose to be going?" I asked.

"Tonight!" Story yelled. "But like I said, he changes faster than the shade."

"Monica!" Daddy yelled. Then he opened the door.

Monica jumped up so fast that I felt a shock from her. She was off and running. As she went inside, Mama came out with an attitude and then told me to come with her. She was pissed about something, and from the excitement in Monica's eyes, I thought I knew what it was.

CHAPTER 5

We were driving in the Cadillac, and since the date was in Michigan City—forty-five minutes away—Mama asked me to roll her up a blunt from the kush sack that she tossed in my lap. Other than that, she hadn't said one word to me, so I sat quietly and rolled a blunt as she drove. She was listening to Sade and drove like a champ, but something was missing.

"You see this?" she asked finally, breaking from her trance. She was showing me a ring on her ring finger.

I nodded and then finished licking the blunt. "That's nice!" I said. What else could I say? She was a ho showing me a wedding ring.

"Do you know that nothing-ass nigga had the nerve to make me remove this when his ex-wife was around? How stupid can a bitch be to put up with that kind of shit? Huh?"

"I'm confused," I admitted. "Is that your wedding ring? Y'all married?"

She giggled and then said, "Let him tell it—I or we or whatever you call it are married to the game. Which makes you and every other bitch that pays him also married to me. My wifey-in-laws!"

I'd heard all of that stuff before about wifey-in-laws and shit, and even heard about the game, but I'd never seen or heard of a bitch having a big-ass diamond ring like the one she was wearing. To be totally frank, it made me jealous. I wanted a ring. I wanted to be a top-notch boss bitch in the game. I wanted *her* ring.

"I'm leaving him!" she said, breaking the moment of silence. It was a large blow.

"Why?"

"This car! That house! Everything is mine! My name is on everything, not his or hers!" she ranted on.

"Monica?"

"Yeah, Monica! That bitch can have him. That bitch got two kids that she pays her baby daddy to babysit just so she can slut for Daddy!" she mimicked. "The bitch has to pay her baby daddy two hundred dollars per week to watch his own sons."

Taken aback, I said, "So why was Monica tripping about my phone?"

"Because she's a jealous piece-of-shit bitch. That bitch is in the way and needs to choose her damn babies over the game."

I was playing Angry Birds on my phone. Deep down inside, I knew that Mama would get over it. The kush was getting to her, and it had a way of calming a bitch down.

The car was nice as hell, but plain. There was a really nice feel to being in the car. The color was baby blue, and it had a white leather interior and enough wood grain in it to make a kitchen table. I took off my heels that Mama gave me to wear. She took good care of me. She was sweet to me. She seemed crazy, don't get me wrong, but for a white bitch, she had class and swagger. The girl drove like she was riding a horse.

By the time we reached the house, I was getting sleepy. I had a long night and then got up early, and before I even got a chance to brush my teeth or wash my ass, I was on my to do a date. I couldn't complain. I did have a new phone. Crazy thing about my phone was it was another bitch's before mine. There was all kinds of tricks stored into it, niggas' pictures, and dick shots! I didn't complain about that neither. Hell, I didn't mind the gifts, and the game that was being ran on me was cool. I couldn't complain.

"Damn! That's a fucking mansion on the ocean!" I blurted out. It looked literally like a house in the movies.

"Girl! Listen to me," she said. "I don't care how nice a crib is, how much jewelry, or how fine a trick is. Never act like you're amazed. If you do, you lose value from the door. It's normal in this game, and all the same tricks see all the bitches, so it's up to you to show them a good time and top-notch service. That way, they become your regulars. Regulars are what this game is all about. Regulars and getting a tip."

We parked. She cut the car off, and we sat in silence. "He know we here?" I asked. The house was pitch black.

"Yeah. His wife must be home, so we wait until he signals for us."

"His wife?" I was staring at her with one eyebrow up. "She's going to kill us, then him."

"Girl, you got so much to learn."

"Will you teach me?" I asked, knowing that so far, she had given me the most game. She even gave me more game than Papa. She was a cold bitch. A true bottom bitch.

"All you got to do is pay attention to everything going on around you. Never cum, but always fake one, and always do your job, with respect!" She stopped and looked into my eyes. "Your heart has to be detached from your pussy. That line has to be drawn from here on out. If you can do all of that, yeah, I will teach you."

"Thank you," I whispered.

"Oh, most importantly! Never go against the game. It's Papa you put your all into. Grimy bitches come and go. It's the game, 'cop and blow,' but he knows them girls before they get here. They come to learn the game and then they go run off."

"That's not me, that's dirty!"

"I know."

"How?" I asked.

"Because Papa put you under my wing. If he didn't like you, he would have put you under Monica."

"Why?" I asked now, feeling like a football getting tossed around.

"Because I breed the best!" she laughed. "Who you think taught that bitch?"

"Who taught Liz?"

"Papa gave the game to Liz," she smiled. There was admiration in her voice. "That bitch been under Monica, me, and Papa."

After she talked so highly of Liz, I knew that was who I wanted to be, and I still hadn't even met her. She sounded like a princess.

The garage door finally opened up, and this old sweet-looking white man about my height came to the door and waved us inside. Mama came to life. She just walked in like she owned the place. There was porn playing on the television, but what got my attention was that there was a picture of me on the computer screen. It was that same picture of me walking up to the car. It was a nice picture, but still, nothing like the way I was looking now. I was embarrassed. These bastards had my real picture on the Internet.

The thought sent resentment into my blood. I felt like, if I didn't even know they had me online, what else didn't I know? They never even asked me.

"So, you are the girl in the picture?" Allen asked me.

"Why wouldn't I be?" I asked, still in a daze.

Mama disappeared into the bathroom. We were not in the big part of the house; instead, the whole garage had been made over into a sex room. This seemed like a secret room that CIA agents would have inside their house, only it was for sex. I don't see how his wife didn't know about something like this.

Then it came to me that if I had a husband and a house this big, not only would I not care, I would even clean up his mess. While waiting for Mama to get done doing whatever it was she was doing in the bathroom, I sat on the sex swing that hung from the ceiling. It was black and leather with a hole at the bottom, both for entrance and for the use of urinating on the client. He was explaining how it worked to me, but I was too busy looking at myself in the mirror from across the room.

"Want to try?" he asked me.

Caught off guard, I said, "Huh?"

"Do you want me to show you how it works?" he asked again in this almost creepy voice.

A chill went up my spine. I didn't even know what to say. I wanted to run or yell for help, but instead I said, "Sure!"

Without hesitation, he got down on his knees. Then he spread my legs apart and lifted my skirt up so that my naked butt and exposed pussy were sitting inside the same seat where maybe a few other escorts had sat before me. In my mind, it felt like going into a public restroom without first gift-wrapping the seat, just hurrying up and plopping down on it. I was smiling—not from joy, but because he was smiling and still on his knees, looking at my pussy. He licked his lips and then spread my legs apart even further. He reached and I jumped, but not from fear. His cold touch reminded me of the first and only other time a white man had touched me there.

"Mmmm," he moaned. Then he took his hard long sticky finger out and smelled it, and then he put it into his mouth and sucked it like it was covered in chocolate. "You taste sweet and fresh."

"Thank you." I gagged. I felt so violated, I could've cried.

"You ready?"

"For what?" I asked, confused. Then I realized. The moment he slid down under the swing, I almost jumped up and ran.

"I'm ready whenever you are!" he said from down below. "Do it!"

Without hesitation, I did. I pissed as hard as I could. I pissed out so hard it hurt.

He used the swing and moved me back and forth so that I could pee all over him. I watched him from the top, and at the sight of him drinking my piss, I couldn't stop myself from throwing up everywhere! All over him, all over the floor! I tried to hold it in, but I couldn't. He didn't even stop until I got done pissing and throwing up.

"I am so sorry," I said, embarrassed. I was done and so was he, but he was not the least bit mad about me tossing up my respect all over him. He was just as sorry as I was.

"Oh, girl, it's okay," Mama said from across the room. She paid me no attention either.

I ran into the bathroom and closed the door behind myself. Tears ran down my face, but I was the only person who shared them with me. I sat in front of the mirror and bawled my eyes out. Once I got done crying, I washed myself up. The sink was huge, and there were towels on the ledge. I grabbed one, and as soon as I opened it up, a crack pipe fell out onto the ground. If it wasn't for the oriental rug it fell on, it would've probably shattered. It was a glass pipe.

Growing up, I remember all of the times I found my mother's pipes around the hotel rooms and places we used to stay. I remembered the smell of burnt metal in the room right after my mother would take a hit. That nightmare was replaying back over in my head, until I was shaken out of my trance by a knock on the door.

"Kassie?" a soft voice said. It was Mama, but it sounded like the voice of my mother so many years before.

"I'm coming, I will be right there," I sniffed. There was no reason to hide my tears. I had uncovered her true identity, and for some strange, odd reason, it made me feel love for her. It made me care.

Nobody is perfect, and for some reason once we realize that under every façade of life lies the person's true self, we start to appreciate those few of us who have the heart to share their story—the heart to help the rest of us see life through their eyes. Mama was, by far, the most beautiful white girl I had ever gotten close to. She had the body of a model. She had a closet so full of nice clothes and a heart as big as a lion. And she had a secret.

I put the pipe back inside the towel and the towel back like I found it. Who cared? It was time to toughen up and go finish what we came to do. I would not let her down. We had a date to do. I looked in the mirror, put back on my fake smile, and then went back to work.

Chapter 6

As soon as we got back to the house, Marcos approached me. "Your brother wants you to call him," he said.

"What did he say?"

Marcos frowned up his nose at me. He was too busy playing a video game to pay me any attention.

"Where is Papa?" Mama asked him. "And can you please turn that down?"

He listened to her but still never looked her or my way to acknowledge either of our presence. "Him and Liz went to have a drink."

"Yeah, fucking right?" Mama snapped. "That bitch must got a room somewhere or some shit. All they ever do is sneak off and fuck every chance they get."

I had nothing to say, even though for some odd reason my heart felt empty and my blood went up a few degrees too. I just went through hell and back over at Allen's house for this man, the least he could do is be here to slap me on my ass or across the face even to tell me "good job." Instead of voicing my opinion, I followed Mama upstairs and jumped straight into the tub. A shower would have been fine too, but since it had been years since I had a chance to sit down in a bathtub, I felt, why not now? The whole time I was locked up, I dreamed of getting out and soaking in a bathtub. A Jacuzzi would've been more accurate, but hell, this was second best.

"Hey bro," I said after he answered the phone. I was still soaking and for once felt relaxed.

"Girl, where have you been? I've been looking for you. Mama been wanting you to come by. What's up?"

"Nothing, bro! I've been chilling."

"Well, keep in touch, girl. I was worried sick about you. I heard you was in Chicago," he said, causing me to want to jump out of the water and go downstairs and kill Marcos, but I was so relaxed, I couldn't move.

"Yeah!" I confessed. Who was I fooling? My brother knew what type of bitch I was, so he knew I would keep it real. "But I was only there for one night. I am back now."

"Oh, before I forget, this white girl called earlier today looking to talk to you and sounded fine as hell."

"What was her name?" I asked. I had given my brother's number to almost all the girls I was locked up in residential with, so it could've been anyone.

"Lindsay, I think," he said and then gave me her number.

My brother loved me to death, but for the last few years, I'd been alone. Deep down inside, I knew I would have to find my way alone again.

After I got out of the shower, Mama gave me a pair of Papa's boxers to wear and showed me how to tie them up with hair ties so they fit my petite ninety-eight-pound frame. The way she talked to me and treated me always made me feel loved. It was crazy, too, because it was like the first time in my life that I felt this way.

"You coming to New York with us?" she asked me. Her iPhone was on the iHome stand playing Sade's "No Ordinary Love" loud enough to wake up the neighborhood.

"I thought we were going to Jersey or Atlantic City, or Pittsburgh somewhere," I replied.

"Who told you that?"

"Story," I told.

"Well, you see, when we run a route, we go everywhere in the area. We going to the east coast. It's all close together. Pittsburgh is on the way."

"Yeah, I would like to go see my son first."

"Where is he?" Mama asked, concerned. Or at least she sounded that way.

Sadly, I said, "He lives with foster parents. I was only sixteen when I had him. I couldn't take care of him on my own."

"You want me to take you to see him? I was adopted too, you know," she said.

"No, I didn't know that. How old were you?"

"I was put in foster care at five but got adopted at eight years old."

"Why?"

"I will tell you about that in due time," she explained. "Just know it was rough for me growing up too."

I couldn't believe my ears. Here I was feeling sorry for myself for the way I was raised, and again I find out I wasn't the only one of us who had been through rough times. Thinking back to when I was a child, I could remember times when I wished I had been saved by a foster parent. There were times when that would've been a dream come true.

"I hated it at first," Mama was saying, "because as far as I knew growing up, I thought the things I went through with my family were normal. It took meeting other girls my age who experienced incest and molestation to realize it was wrong," she said, her tears matching mine. "Once I finally found a family, my world changed. That was the best thing that ever happened to me."

Mama might have been talking to me about her experience, but deep down, I understood the reason behind all that she said. My son, Carlton, was happy. No matter if I raised him or not, his being happy meant more to me than my own happiness.

I was stretched across the king-size bed thinking about my own happiness when Papa finally came in the room. Again, he paid me no attention. He walked up behind Mama and wrapped his arms around her in a way that made me want to scream.

I was dying for some affection. I'd lived my whole life and never had anything that was real. Even with my baby daddy, it wasn't real, because I was so much younger than him it felt like he was molesting me every time we had sex. What we did to make Carlton was wrong, and he and I both knew it when I got pregnant. I was only fifteen years old.

"She wants to see her son before we go out east," Mama said. Her tone was pleading, as if she knew he couldn't care less but she also knew the importance.

"We can't!" he said, grabbing some boxers, a brand new pack of socks, and some V-neck tees. Then he said, "We leaving ASAP. She can see him when we get back. The route is only going to take a week. It's not that serious, I know."

Mama looked over at me. I played like I was asleep. Really, I played sleep because my eyes were so full of tears. He couldn't care less about my son. Who was I fooling? He was a pimp!

I stayed there with my eyes closed long enough to fall asleep. By the time I was fully awake again, we were driving east on the toll road. I was still wearing his boxers. I was scared. It was like I was leaving my world behind, and I still did not know what existed. Was this my fate? I just wanted to see my son. Who cared where I ended up?

We were all riding in a black conversion van. I thought it was going to be a bunch of us, but it wasn't—only me, Story, Monica, Marcos, Mama, and Papa. I was glad. These were my favorites of all the girls. Even though they all were jealous, I'd talked to them before, and for some odd reason it just felt better to have Marcos there.

CHAPTER 7

Pittsburgh was beautiful! Marcos drove the entire way. It took about six and a half hours to get there. The whole way, I played Angry Birds on my phone. I swear we probably smoked ten blunts of kush. It was late, so the scenery full of mountains and bridges, going inland and crossing the river, was very nice. There were lights all over the bridges and on the ferries that sailed up the river.

In the distance, I saw the Rivers Casino, and then there was Heinz Stadium spreading out across the backdrop of the city. The baseball stadium was lit up as we drove by, and there was a live game going on and playing on the extremely large screen. It was amazing!

"Cuz, where we staying this time?" Marcos asked

Papa, searching for a location on the GPS, said, "I don't know yet."

"Want me to go over to the Comfort Suites on Bankersville Road?"

"Papa, you know the police know that's our spot," Mama said. "Last time we was there, everybody got locked up." She was doing her makeup in the letdown mirror.

"Bitch, don't tell me how to do my job!"

"Sorry!" she snapped back. "I am just saying. Why not go out to Monroeville? The Red Roof Inn or Days Inn?"

Papa didn't respond. Instead, he put the address in the GPS. Next thing you know, we were at the Days Inn. I will never forget the bar behind our room. It smelled so good from the huge barbecue grill that smoked some of the best-smelling food. The rooms, however, were disgusting. Our room was on the bottom floor, which was weird because the lobby was on the second floor. Everything about Pittsburgh was different because all the buildings seemed to have been built inside the mountains.

Mama and Papa had a single bedroom next door to our room. It had a king-size bed and a flat-screen in it, and it was nonsmoking. I wished I could stay in the room with them. Marcos jumped all up in one of the beds, took his shoes off, and stunk up the whole room. Monica and Story claimed the only free bed, pretty much leaving me no choice but to sleep with Marcos. I stood by the door looking for something, anything, to do besides sitting or laying in the bed, so I decided to go ahead and soak in the tub. For some reason, being out of town with them made me feel alone again—almost like it felt when we were all locked up in JJC. There were over a hundred girls all in the same dorm, but all doing time separately and for separate reasons.

I laid in this tub not because I felt the need to clean myself up, but because it was the only place I could think. This game was so different from the way I always expected life to be as a prostitute. Growing up, I always thought I did dates for a way to eat. Now, on the road, I wanted to do a date just to escape this room. I want to do a date to get more attention.

"Kassie!" Story yelled, while at the same time knocking at the door, hard as hell, waking me from my daydream. "Hurry up!"

"Okay! Chill the fuck out!"

"You chill the fuck out, bitch!" she snapped instantly, causing my blood to rise.

Instead of reacting to her outburst, I took my sweet time. I'd been called plenty of bitches by the girls I was locked up with. *Bitch* is just a code name for all women. It's just the way Papa said *bitch*. He had a lethal way of saying *bitch* that cut so deep that no matter who he was talking to, it felt like he was talking to us all.

By the time I got out of the tub and got dressed—again in the same dress and outfit that Mama gave me on day one—it was time to go on a date. Marcos was driving, and me and everybody but Mama and Papa rode out.

"This is some bullshit," Story said from the front seat. For some reason, it felt like she was doing little things to get under my skin. Jumping in the front seat, harassing me while I was trying to get myself off, and calling me all types of bitches was her way of messing with me. Little did she know, I couldn't care less about that front seat. For all I cared, she could sleep with his musty ass too!

"What you tripping about now?" Marcos asked her all flirtatiously. He was trying to make me jealous, but little did they both know, I wanted to be up in the front seat all night but with Papa Bear driving, and us two the only people in the car.

"Why the fuck we got to always get sent off?"

"Girl, chill out!" Monica jumped in. She had been quiet for most of the trip. Her eye was a little swollen from getting slapped, and her lip was a little messed up too, but she didn't seem to care. She looked as if she was glowing. She looked like she was happy. She was the only one of us who had a date to go to, which I understood was Story's point.

"That's easy for you to say, because you the only bitch getting dicked down."

"Fuck you!" Monica laughed. "I get my ass whooped all the time too."

"You like it!"

"Call it what you like."

I sat in the very back of the van and listened to how stupid these crazy-ass bitches sounded. Marcos paid them no attention either. I could tell he heard plenty of these conversations and wondered if he ever told Papa what they be saying. Who cares?

We rode all around Pittsburgh, Greensburgh, Wilkinsburgh, and Greentree. By the time we got back to the room, it was nine o'clock in the morning. I had done four dates, each for three hundred dollars, and almost everybody gave me a tip too. Pittsburgh was a gold mine. I never would've thought it would be so many dates to do.

Story only did one date, and it was only for a hundred and fifty. She had an attitude with me, and I thought I knew why. I was the one who pulled her in on one of my dates with me. She didn't even want to do it either, because it was at a hotel downtown, but it was three guys, and I fucked two at the same time. Crazy as it was, it was the most fun I'd ever had while having sex. Them guys loved me. They were visiting for the baseball game and drunk as hell. They even had a kush for me. I had a blast!

Only thing about the whole night that made me wonder was the smell of sex and the condom wrapper I found on the floor inside the van. Something wasn't right. Either way, I knew it wasn't me, but somebody was fucking Marcos behind Papa's back. Looking at both Story and Monica, I had no clue which one or what I'd missed.

CHAPTER 8

After a couple hours' rest, we were being woke up by housekeeping. The fact that we hadn't been to sleep didn't matter to them. Instead of paying for the room for another night, we packed up and went back down to Wilkinsburg to shop at the Rainbow that was on the main strip.

Wilkinsburg was ghetto with a capital *G*. The main strip was Broad Street, or the "8," as Papa called it. After we all shopped, we went to Papa's favorite sandwich spot, called Peppi's. The food was good, too. I ordered a boilermaker sandwich because Papa ordered the boilermaker salad, which was huge! It was full of meats and the craziest thing I'd ever seen. It was topped with French fries!

"Who puts fries on top of their salad?" I asked Papa. He was sharing with Mama. She didn't order anything. The restaurant was in an old trailer, it seemed; it was small but packed. Wilkinsburg was all black, and we stood out! It seemed like everybody knew we were out-of-towners and prostitutes.

"Want to try?" Mama asked, holding her fork for me to take a bite after her. I was fatigued—we all were, except Mama. She seemed well rested.

I took the bite. Funny, because I never shared with anyone growing up, not even my own mother. Mama treated me different from how she treated everyone else. I didn't know if it was because I was new or what. I just knew it made me feel pointed out, targeted. "Thank you!" I said.

"Heard you did good last night," she said under her breath. Everybody else was sitting in a booth at a distance, except Marcos. He went down to McDonald's. All he ate was chicken nuggets, plain. I thought that was weird.

"I did okay," I told Mama.

"You did better than okay. Let Papa tell it. Seems like you made the most money last night," she said in a joking but serious voice. It was more of a warning than anything.

"I didn't . . . did I?"

"It doesn't really matter," Papa said through a mouthful of salad and ranch dressing. Usually the sight of a person talking with a mouthful of food would make my stomach turn, but with him, it was cute. Everything about him was cute to me. "Tonight we will be working Carson Street by Station Square downtown. That's where we will see what you're made of. You did do good, though."

"Thank you," I said, with butterflies turning inside my stomach. I couldn't eat another bite of my food. It wasn't the fact that tonight we would be out working the track or ho stroll, it was that if it was true that I made the most money last night, then I would be getting dicked down by Papa.

Really, I don't even know if dick is what I wanted from him. I really would rather be held. I'd had enough dick last night to last a couple of days.

I looked up and my eyes met Papa's. It seemed he was inside my head, reading my mind. He made me nervous. I took another chewy bite and said, "I need something done to my hair, and my nails need to get done."

The table got quiet. Maybe the whole restaurant was silent for a moment. Then he said, "If we wait until we get to Jersey, we can go to midtown in Elizabeth. I know this spot off Broad that do nails for twenty-five dollars a set, both feet and hands!"

"That's when? Tomorrow? Next week? If you want me to go out and work the track looking all crazy, then I can just go home," I said. I couldn't believe my own words. I mean, maybe the restaurant full of strangers made me feel more at home. I knew, deep down inside my heart, that if I walked away from them, I could meet somebody who would help me get home. "I'm not going out anywhere then."

"Girl, you need to chill out," Mama snapped.

"This ain't got shit to do with you," I warned.

"Bitch, step!" Papa yelled. The whole room was now aware of our situation. "Take your funky ass on then."

"Sir!" the middle-aged waiter said, loud enough for everybody who was listening to hear. "You all need to leave."

Without another word, embarrassed, I got up. The waiter looked at me, I looked at him, and then I looked back at Papa. "Okay, you want me to leave?" He didn't look up. I left.

Outside, the streets looked much more scary. I knew I had to leave, but I didn't know which way to run. Either way would do.

"Where you going?" Marcos yelled. I wanted to run. The van was in the parking lot, but Marcos was sitting next to it, on the curb, eating, taking pictures of graffiti.

"Take me home!"

"What?" he said. He didn't want to hear anything I had to say. I could tell he had seen this all before. I took off running. Marcos chased me. I didn't know why, but for the first time since the beginning of the trip, I was glad to have him around. The horns blew, my phone fell, but I kept running.

"Kassie!" he yelled. The cars that saw Marcos chasing me all tried to stop me too. One pulled into the Walgreen's parking lot. It was a red Cadillac that had rims on it, with a younger-looking brother inside of it.

"Help!" I yelled.

The door of his car swung open on the passenger side. I jumped in, not realizing that there were two girls in the backseat. They were both young too, and scared—not of Marcos, but of me. We pulled off . . . fast!

"Is that your boyfriend?" the driver asked me. He was smiling, exposing the gold teeth in his mouth.

"Drop me off at the bus stop," I demanded.

"You got some money?" he asked me while at the same time taking his eyes off the road and pulling a big bankroll from his pocket to flaunt in my face.

"I do not have any money, but I know how to get it. I will be fine."

"Don't look that way to me. Looks like you could use some of my sucker repellant." He laughed in a phony way. "Bitch, show this bitch how we get rid of the suckers."

Both the girls pulled out pepper spray. They were both cute; they almost looked like they could be sisters. The one behind the driver was young, maybe fifteen or sixteen, while the other one looked a year or so older. You could tell they both were underage but seasoned, as if they could've been raised by the streets.

"You can have this one," the younger, prettier one said, handing me the spray. She was light-skinned, more red than brown, and had a huge rack on her chest, squeezed by the skimpy shirt she had on showing off cleavage.

"Thank you!" I said. I knew he was a pimp, even though he said nothing about it to me. I could see it in the girls' eyes, almost a warning to escape while I still could. Besides, mace would come in handy, especially if I planned on trying to hustle up enough money to make it home.

We pulled up to the Greyhound station. It was a relief, but not really. I mean, yeah, for a second I was worried about getting kidnapped. Now, looking at the crowd at the bus station, I kind of wished I had been. The driver handed me a fifty-dollar bill, but before releasing it into my hand, he said, "Look, you don't have to go home. You more than welcome to go home with us."

I thought about it. Honestly, I did. Of course, I didn't know them. Neither did I know anyone else I was with. Marcos was the most I knew out of everybody, and so far as phone numbers go, the only number I knew was my own. "No, thank you," I said. Then I snatched the money from his hand, noticing the pretty hazel eyes he had.

He handed me his business card. I read it, and to my surprise it was for some exotic call-girl service called Secret Service. *Anytime, Anywhere.*

I got out of the car and then looked and realized it was nice as hell, maybe even brand new. Papa's caddy was nice, but this one was a pretty red with huge rims and tires and a navigation system in it.

As he pulled away, the younger girl jumped back up in the front seat. She blew me a kiss, and I blew one back. I wondered what life would've been like if I would have stayed in that car. I may have really been meant to meet them. Not to mention, the driver looked sexy as hell. Even better than Papa.

I went straight to the pay phone and dialed my number. A stranger picked up on the first ring. It was some dude who had seen me running. He came straight to the station and gave the phone back in exchange for my number. He was also sexy. Young, same gold teeth, but a white boy. I mean, from the slang in his super-sexy voice to the Escalade truck he pulled up in, I could've sworn he was a baller. I gave him my number. He pulled off.

"Hello," I answered the phone when it rang a few minutes later. I knew it was him. I smiled. Not because he answered, but because in the parking lot I saw the van pull up with Marcos's head sticking all out the window. I paid them no attention, even though I really was glad to see them. Papa was alone walking toward me. This would be the second time we ever had a conversation alone. He walked up as if he had not a care in the world. His eyes were bloodshot red from the kush weed I had given him the night before. This man walking toward me made my blood boil. He had true swag, the swag of a pimp. The way he dressed, talked, and acted was all pimpin'. I wondered if all pimps were this way.

"Where the fuck are you going?" he asked me in a cold threatening voice, but his demeanor was opposite. He hugged me for the crowd. I hugged him back, but I really wish I had run away. I couldn't, not from him. Not ever. He was a magnet. He jerked me, hard. Then he looked me in the eyes. A tear fell.

"Here!" I shook out of my quivering lips. I gave him the fifty-dollar bill that the driver had given me. He took it and immediately put it into his pocket.

"Let me see that," he said, snatching my phone. The screen was cracked, but not to the point that I couldn't see that someone was on the phone. "Hello? Hello?"

I was still in his arms, shaking to the point of pissing on myself, like an excited puppy dog. "I want to go home," I said.

"Bitch, you ain't going no fucking where. I should knock your funky ass to the ground and put this size thirteen on ya!"

For some reason, I believed him. I was even a little turned on by the fact that he wanted me there with him. "Don't hit me!"

"What?" he yelled, balling his fist up and raising his hand up as if he would swing.

The people around us paid no attention. They were too busy looking at the van where Mama was yelling to Papa, "Slap yourself, bitch, and then get your once-a-month, funky, cock-bleeding ass on the roof of that van, so I can ride around town and let the state of Pennsylvania smell my toes as they stick out of the crack of your ass."

I tried not to laugh. I couldn't believe my ears. This motherfucker was crazy to think I would slap myself. Who the fuck he think he is? But I did. I slapped myself so hard I saw black and blue flashes in my eyes. "Is this what you want?"

"Now get the fuck in the van, bitch!" he yelled back, matching my tone. Tears stung the side of my face as they rolled down. I let them roll all the way to the van. Papa stayed outside cursing at Mama. Then they both got in, and we pulled off like we never had any issues.

Marcos passed me the blunt. Then he smirked to Papa. They both exchanged smiles, and so did Story and Monica, but Mama got all the way in the backseat of the van and wrapped her arms around me. I cried my eyes out. I needed her so much. I let all of the tears flow freely out onto her lap, and she just rubbed me until I felt calm. I was tired and heartbroken by a man I barely knew.

Papa did something to me. I don't even know what it was, just that he believed in me. Then there was Mama. I think her loyalty and dedication are what made me stay. I couldn't leave her out here. Not now, not ever.

"Look," Mama said. It was straight to the point. "I've been where you sit now. I know how you feel."

"How?" I cried through the sniffles.

"I was not always his bitch," she said. The way she said *bitch* was weird to me. It was, to her, a title like *wife*, but from the outside looking in, she sounded crazy.

"What you mean?" I asked.

"Just like I said," she told me, forcing me to sit up. The girls were listening, but Papa and Marcos couldn't hear anything. Sade's "Soldier of Love" was playing. It matched the mood I was in, so I chilled out. "When I first met him, he was married. I worked for him and his wife. They had an escort service, mostly bitches that got high, because Papa sold crack. He was ballin', too! I mean, I ain't going to lie, I was getting high when I met Papa. He never even looked at me. One time I told him that I would become his number one, and he laughed."

We stopped at a house and Papa got out. There were about five handsome-looking niggas outside, showing Papa love. Then he went inside. Marcos changed the music soon as Papa jumped out. All he did was complain about the music collection.

"What happened to his wife?" I asked. I knew it sounded stupid, but I wanted to know, maybe even understand.

"She left him. Out of the blue. Told him she was going to the store and never came home," Mama said, sounding as if she felt sorry for him, but I don't think so. I saw a different picture.

"Did she know about y'all?" I asked.

"We wasn't together-together then. One day, I stopped by they house to get some shit, and he was curled up in the bed like he couldn't move."

"Damn . . . what was wrong with him?"

"He just couldn't get up. It had been days. There was a party going on, a few of his customers running around drinking the beer up, clowning, and having a crack party. I met most of them through him, so I stayed. I partied. I just never left."

"Just like that?" I asked.

"Well, it was more to it than that. He had a lady named Karrie Joe trying to set up dates on one of the service lines, and I took over the line and closed the dates. His wife used to set up all the calls. It wasn't easy, either. Them weirdos used to ask me all these weird questions."

"Like what?" I asked interested.

"Like BBJs, which means a bareback blow job; or Greek, which means anal; or multipops, which means to pay for an hour but cum several times," she said. "If you don't know what you're doing, they will have you agreeing to all kinds of shit and not knowing what you are walking into."

Papa got back into the car with a bag full of pills. It was ecstasy, and I was ready to pop off for the first time. I took one, and so did everybody else in the car.

Chapter 9

Our rooms were at the Sheridan Hotel in Station Square. It was really nice, too. The view from our room was off the river. It was really beautiful looking across the river to all the downtown buildings and bridges lit all up. I could see the highway that we drove in on but the opposite side.

The pill was working its way through my body now. Even though I was the first one dressed, I was the last one to leave the room. I was still embarrassed. I had on a red dress. It was very elegant, with a black wrap to cover my arms that matched my black pump heels. I had a black clutch and a bunch of cheap jewelry that Rainbow sells three for $5.99. I looked nice, but for the first time I felt cheap. My cheek was swollen up from me slapping myself, and my self-esteem had taken a dive.

Marcos, Story, and Monica went down to Dave and Buster's. They all seemed to be having an extra fun time. Me, on the other hand—I felt like jumping into the river from this top floor, even not knowing how to swim.

"You cool?" Papa asked, walking into our room with his key. The fact that he had a key to our room while him and Mama had their own made me feel like a hostage.

"I am rolling like that river," I told him, trying to play it cool, but really I wanted to cry. He knew it, too. "Where is Mama?"

"She got a date coming upstairs in a minute," he said.

"I thought we don't do in-calls here in Pittsburgh?" I asked, still with my eyes glued to the window and view. For some reason, I couldn't face him. He was sitting at the table rolling up a blunt.

"You don't do in-calls because you are new to the game still, but once you get experience and learn the script, then you will be able to know a trick from the law. What you think Mama was doing last night?"

"I don't know!" I admitted. "Laid up with you?"

"You're crazy," he laughed, setting the blunt down and walking up behind me. Then he whispered into my ear, sending a chill through my body, "I don't lay up."

We left it at that. He was so close to me; I was shaking so hard I couldn't speak. The pill was running through my body so hard I couldn't help the sweat forming on my brow. The moment he touched my shoulder and turned me around to face him, I almost threw up. The feeling reminded me of the girls I was locked up with when they explained how they were raped and molested as children growing up. I was ready to scream because I didn't want him to touch me.

"You look really nice," he said, but now in a more seductive tone—almost a softer voice. Maybe he knew how I must have felt. He touched me again, but this time he grabbed my hand and pulled me toward him.

"Thank you," I said, blushing. Maybe it was the pill or the mixed feelings or even the game, but all of a sudden I wanted him to kiss me. He didn't. "You look nice too!"

He had on a black-and-white prison-striped tight-fitting shirt that exposed his belly, some black capri pants, black-and-white alligator shoes, and some black-and-white striped socks to match. He looked like one of those mimes you see with their faces painted, performing at a carnival and not speaking. He even had the hat to match. Honestly, he looked ridiculous, but in a very cute way. His shoes alone cost more than all of our outfits put together.

"Are you going to be okay tonight?" he asked in that same hypnotizing soft voice while gently rubbing my arm up to my shoulder. The pill was kicking in, my heart was racing, and my pussy was getting wet.

"Yes," I whispered back, not fully understanding what it was I was agreeing to. Not really caring either—all I wanted was his touch. Maybe I even felt like it was the least he could do.

My eyes were rolling back in my head. My hands were somewhere. I had no control of myself. He started with gentle kisses on my neck but quickly pulled the front of my dress down, barely ripping it but turning me on so much my hands found the buckle of his pants at the same time that his mouth covered my breast. I couldn't compare the insatiable feeling to anything else. As he sucked and nibbled at my nipple, I reached and stroked his dick softly. We moaned together.

"I want you inside me," I heard myself say, although I had no control of the words as they came out of my mouth. Instead of waiting for him to reply, I dropped down to my knees and took him into my mouth. He tasted sweet, like he had flavored lotion all over his body.

He moaned in that same voice he spoke to me in, and it made me want him even more. This was driving me crazy! I wanted to please him, pay him, and honestly, I wanted to run away with him. Crazy part is, I didn't know why. All of a sudden, his legs started to shake. He was giving in. The thought of me being able to make this giant of a man fall weak at the knees made me suck harder and harder. I wanted him to scream my name out. He was moaning so hard and shaking uncontrollably. Then he came. I can't explain how it made me feel, because him cumming inside of my mouth made my pussy feel like he was cumming inside of me. I swallowed every last drop. I could taste the margaritas he drank up all day. The taste of his pimp juice was so much better than an ice-cold glass of lemonade on a hot summer day. It quenched my thirst the same way.

I fixed his pants back up for him. I can't lie, deep down inside I was hoping he wouldn't run straight into the bathroom to wash himself up. I cleaned him up perfectly and wanted to leave my scent on him. I know this sounds petty, but let me tell you that when you're dealing with a pimp who is dealing with several different women all day long, every little bit counts, and something so small as that makes you feel good about yourself.

After he looked me up and down without saying anything, he picked up the blunt and sat down. I think he wanted to say something, but he didn't. Instead, he lit up the blunt.

"You know this is a nonsmoking room, Daddy?" Monica said as soon as she entered the room. She was alone and barged in like she was the police.

"Do I really give a fuck?" he said, back to his harsh ways. Just seeing how he went from a puppy poodle to a full-grown pit bull in an instant made me melt.

"Okay, but when they charge us $250 again, don't be saying I've been smoking in the room," she said, knowing that I knew she had been smoking in the room already. They all did. I was the only one who didn't, but I took a hit of the blunt when Papa passed it to me.

Monica looked at me like a cobra snake about to strike its prey. It was almost like, *Move over, bitch, or get out the room.* I rolled my eyes back at her and then tried to hand her the blunt, but she refused it from me. I gave it to Papa.

"When we leaving?" she asked. "I am ready to work!"

"Where is Marcos and Story?"

Instead of answering his question, Monica made a mischievous face, almost telling on them but not really. Even though Papa acted like he got the point, he didn't say anything. I guess it explained the empty condom wrapper.

After we smoked the blunt, it was time to go. Mama was done with her date, so we all met up in the van. I can't lie, my adrenaline was pumping. I wasn't scared, more like excited.

Everyone in the car acted like this was going to be the time when I failed. I think everyone except Papa thought I would. Little did they know, I started off on the stroll.

"Look!" Papa said. He was driving down Carson. There were bars everywhere on both sides of the road. College kids were up and down the blocks, music was playing from the clubs, and the smell of food was in the air. "When we park, we will be on 17th Avenue and Carson. I will be parked in the parking lot so you can always know where the van is. Mama, you and Monica are going to walk toward 22nd Street. I will be at Burger King, online, where I can see you two. So walk across at 17th and stop at every bar along the way and have a drink. Once you get to Rite Aid, cross back over. Then do the same, but stop at the barbecue spot and grab me a rib dinner."

"Can I get some ribs too, Daddy?" Monica asked. She just wanted to be heard.

"No, grab a slice of cheese pizza once you drop off my ribs. This ain't no fucking vacation, bitch. Your messy, nasty ass going to get barbecue sauce all over that white dress," he laughed. "What type of ho wears white on the track?"

"Why you so mean to me all the time?" she asked all sad, but not really. She was enjoying the attention.

"Bitch, shut the fuck up with that weak-ass shit," he snapped. "Now all of a sudden your funky ass can't take a joke?"

"I was just kidding, dang," she said.

Marcos was cracking up as he was parking. He was enjoying himself a little bit too much, while Story was quiet as a mouse.

"Kassie, you and Story going to walk this side of the street, but in the opposite direction. I want y'all to walk all the way down to 9th and then switch sides and come back up the block," he explained. "Now, I want you two to hold hands the whole way. Once you get past 11th, it's going to be more of a hip-hop black crowd, so be careful down there. Don't lose each other. No niggas, you hear me?"

I heard him, but Story had an attitude. "I will talk to a nigga if he got some money."

Before she could get the words out of her mouth good, Papa was reaching back trying to snatch her up. She knew it was coming, too, so she jumped into the backseat where I was sitting.

"Bitch, don't make me send you out of this van black and blue."

She didn't say anything, just readjusted herself and got back in her seat. Papa seemed like he wanted more, but he left it alone. The car was silent except for Marcos, who was still giggling, but not like it was funny.

"Let me out! Y'all trippin'," Mama said. She hadn't said one word so far; she was ready to go and knew how to. Monica was on her heels. At first I wondered why Papa told us to hold hands but not them, but I decided it would be better to keep my mouth shut. We got out last.

Soon as we got out of the van, Story came to life. She talked to everybody who walked past us, mostly niggas too, and gave her number to anybody and everybody who would take it. This way of working the track didn't make any sense to me, because I was used to getting picked up and offered twenty dollars. She was telling everybody five hundred to a thousand for us both, and surprisingly they all agreed to calling us after the bars closed.

"If these guys agreeing to spending time with us later, why not leave now and go get they money?" I asked her. She was having fun, so it seemed. We had guys pull up into bars and buy us drink after drink, and neither one of us was twenty-one.

"This is called *traditional*," she said. "There are tracks that you can go on the spot, like Vegas or Miami Beach, but out here and in college towns, you don't have the luxury of places being open 24/7, so you need to cover as much ground as you can while you can. I would hate to leave with two guys who want to spend five hundred and be with them for a couple hours, and then when we get back out here, everything will be closed."

"That makes sense, I guess," I said. "But what if we get all these numbers and nobody wants us later?"

"Watch!" she laughed, looking me in my eyes to get my complete attention. "That's why we get they numbers, too, because they will get drunk and forget, but watch how many be ready afterward. I doubt we have enough time to get to all of them. Daddy knows what he is doing. Just smile and have fun. We'll have plenty of work to do later on."

I did just that. Story was good at this, too. This girl I was walking with was totally different from the girl I met earlier. She was good at working the track. Even if I tried to deny it, I was learning a lot from her. Guys were all over her, too. They hardly paid me any attention. Several of them fawned all over her, and she just smiled as if it was nothing. She was the only one of us who didn't have on a dress. She wore a pair of fishnet pantyhose with some black leather-looking shorts, a black bustier-type pushup bra, and a black wrap around, just like the one I had on. If we looked like dykes, she definitely looked like the bitch of the two.

Chapter 10

The next day, we were back on the road again. It seemed like, from all the money we made in Pittsburgh, we should've stayed. I was tired, my pussy was swollen, and my feet were cut up and hurt from all that walking I did in those heels.

Everybody in the car was asleep. Marcos was driving, I was in the front seat, Monica was laying on the floor of the van with a Mickey Mouse blanket, and Mama and Papa both were asleep on the fold-out bed in the back. I was jealous—but really not because I wasn't in the back laying on top of Papa's chest, but because I didn't make the most money last night.

What really made me sick was the fact that Story and I pulled in the most dates just like she said we would, but because we were so busy, we referred the ones we couldn't get to to Mama and Monica, and the one guy I met who I knew was going to be a good trick spent fifteen hundred with Mama, and she only spent a couple hours with him at that. I was pissed, because I was doing two guys and licking Story's nasty pussy for only three hundred while Mama was with my fish.

Just the thought of it gave me a bad taste in my mouth, along with the sore throat I somehow or other accumulated overnight. Now we were back on the road, and I still hadn't taken a shower or brushed my teeth. We left at the break of dawn at short notice, so the taste in my mouth along with my bad breath made me scared to speak.

"Cuz!" Marcos yelled loudly over the music. He had been rude the whole trip. It seemed like he was driving recklessly ever since we had been on the road, trying to wake us up. Then on top of all that, he kept the music blazing out the front speakers, only with the rear speakers off so that Papa could sleep.

"What's up?" Papa yelled back.

Pretty much everybody in the car was still sleeping. I was up now and looking at the "Welcome to New Jersey" sign as we drove in. Jersey was pretty and bright. I always pictured Jersey being a real city-like environment, but from the looks of the scenery, it was very green. It was full of big old trees and highways. You could tell the difference between being in Pennsylvania and Jersey because it went from hilly mountains to flat land, and it seemed like the weather changed, too.

"Want me to stop over off the 1 and 9 in Elizabeth on Floral and Anna to get some piff?" Marcos asked. I think he was showing off for me, kind of letting me know where he was going. For some reason, it seemed like he was trying to impress me.

"Yeah, but pull up to a gas station first. We need to grab a dutch."

"What's that?" I asked Marcos. I was trying to be nice to him, even though it wasn't easy.

"A vanilla dutch is what they smoke the piff out of around here," he said.

"What's piff?"

"Piff is another word for haze or exotic," he told me, loving to hear his own voice. "We call it doodie or dro. Out here they call it piff."

We stopped at the gas station off the main highway 1 and 9. This gas station was about a dollar cheaper than it was on the road. I knew, because ever since we'd been on the road, I'd paid close attention to how much money we spent on gas and food—so far, over a thousand dollars, and that's just if I included fast food. Once you figure in the drinks and drugs, hell, and the clothes, we might of spent a couple thousand or more.

We pulled up to the gas station, but it didn't look like one. It looked like it was a Laundromat from the outside. Unless my eyes were deceiving me, it was definitely a Laundromat.

These Indian-looking guys were standing in a booth between each set of pumps. When one of them walked up to the van, I almost screamed at how much cash he held in his hand. He was standing in the middle of the parking lot counting what seemed to be thousands on top of thousands of dollars. I looked around at the crowd, and another Indian-looking guy was doing the same. He was counting just as much if not more and couldn't have been any more than fifteen years old.

Nobody seemed to notice but me. There were rough-looking guys around the way who paid us no attention either. Where I was from, in South Bend, Indiana, people got less money robbing banks. They would walk clean up and blow both of these Indians' heads off for this amount of money.

After we got our gas pumped, we went to get the piff. Now, this neighborhood was rough. There were guys standing out on the blocks selling drugs openly. I had never seen anything like it before in my life. It kind of reminded me of a DMX video I'd seen once, because almost everybody had pit bulls tied to chairs.

We parked on the block right on the corner of Flora and Jackson. I will never forget the corner, because I had to remember where the van was parked at and get out and walk to get a dutch. Story jumped up and ran with me—maybe to not let me go alone, but most likely to see the niggas up close. She loved dread heads. They were everywhere you looked.

"Let me get that for you, lovely ladies," this really fine light-skinned brother with long pretty hair said. "You not from around here, are you?"

"No, just passing through," I said. He was all up in my face smiling. He had big strong arms like he'd been working out or in prison. As I let him hold the door open for us, I said, "Thank you!"

"You are more than welcome. So what brings you to the hard part of Elizabeth?"

I was looking for something to drink in the cooler. Story was too, but she was also staring and smiling at him. "A dutch!" I said, sounding lame.

"What you know about dutches?" he joked. Then he pulled out a baggy full of little glass valves of weed or piff, I should say. There were about twenty or more of them, but he also had smaller glass valves that were tied up in bundles of ten.

"Are you going to give that to me?" I asked

"All this?" he joked. "No, but I tell you what. If you give me your number, I will give you one to try out."

I thought about it for a minute, but then I decided not to give my number to him. Papa would kill me. "I can't give you my number, but you can give me yours, and I promise I will call."

He looked me up and down, and then he asked, "Why you can't give me your number? You got a man?"

I wanted to tell him I had a man, but it wouldn't come out. "I have a pimp."

"A pimp?" he sarcastically asked, half-surprised, but turned on by the fact. "What a fine little petite honey like yourself need a pimp for?"

Story was embarrassed. She took her apple Snapple and headed for the van, leaving me behind. I let her go. I felt tension from her, but now I knew she was hating me for being loyal to the game.

"Look, I got to go! If you give me your number, I will call," I told him. "But first . . ."

He looked down at my hand and smiled at me. Then he took out two of the piff valves and gave them to me. Then he handed me a business card from his back pocket.

I thought to myself about everybody carrying business cards around out here on the east coast. I put the card inside my clutch and hurried to catch up with Story.

"Why you walk off like that?" I asked.

She didn't break stride but slowed down her pace. "You don't have to be all uppity and shit, telling him you're a ho. How do you think it made me look?"

"My bad, I didn't know we kept that a secret," I told her. The van was coming up, and there was four niggas hanging out talking to Papa like long-lost friends.

"It's nothing to be proud of . . ." she said as she finally perked up and put on her little fake smile and slut walk. She was so funny.

The guys all looked us up and down as we jumped back into the van. Story gave Papa her Snapple apple and then got up in the front seat again. This bitch was on my last nerve. Every chance she got, she did little things to get under my skin. All she wanted was all the attention, and the front two windows were lightly tinted just enough for her to be nosy.

Papa opened the front door of the van and let one of the guys look in. He looked over to the backseat but pretty much all he saw was me, because Monica and Mama were still asleep. Then he looked back at Story, who was smiling at him and happy like she already knew what time it was.

"You!" he said. His voice was raspy; his beard was huge but clean-cut. It made Rick Ross's beard look small. His head was shaved bald.

"Come on," Papa told her.

"Where we going?" she asked, hesitating just a little bit.

He handed her back her Snapple after first taking a gulp the size of half the bottle. "You might need this, and hurry up, too. We got to check into the hotel early enough so we can get a free night."

"Wait a minute! Where am I going?"

"Bitch, get the fuck out of the van and go!" he yelled, snatching her by her hair. Then he reached in to grab some rubbers out of the glove box;

they were thin Trojans and Magnums. "I am surprised we still got some of these. You might need them!"

He tossed the rubbers at her feet and then got up in the front seat. She was scared, but it didn't show. Instead, she just went with the flow and got into a little beat-up abandoned car that was parked in front of us. They both got in the backseat.

I couldn't believe my eyes or ears. What was so messed up is, I wondered what I would've done if he had chosen me. I was scared of the thought, but I didn't feel sorry for Story. She was getting treated the way she acted.

I handed the piff I had gotten to Papa but kept the business card to myself. Papa looked at me with piercing eyes but didn't say anything. Instead, he handed one of the valves to Marcos so he could roll it up.

"Where is Story?" Mama asked, waking up.

"She is doing a car date," Papa told her, keeping his eyes on the car that Story was in.

"Papa, can you come back here and hold me?" she said. She talked like a little baby to him. It was cute but sickening. I wondered if he would've made Mama go if the guy had chosen her.

It didn't take long at all before Story came back to the van. She was crying like a baby, more embarrassed than anything. She got in the back with Mama, and instantly Mama wrapped her up in a hug.

"Bitch, ain't nothing wrong with you. Shut the fuck up!"

"I hate you!" Story screamed. "I hope you die!"

"Good."

"You a evil monster!" she said, but as she said it, spit came out of her mouth and snot came out of her nose. She burst into laughter. She put her head down and tried to play it off, but it was too late. We all laughed with her.

Deep down, nothing was funny. The game wasn't funny. This girl was fighting for attention and getting it. I was stuck in a war with her, basically fighting for the number-three spot in the car, not to mention in his life, because he was still working Liz in Chicago on the weekends.

He talked on the phone with Liz all day long. If they wasn't talking, they were texting each other. It was really sickening, because this bitch wasn't even around and got more attention than I did. Something had to give, and I knew that in order to get his attention, I had to make room the hard way.

CHAPTER 11

We got a couple of rooms at the Swan Hotel right on the 1 and 9 in Linden, New Jersey. Linden was the next town over from Elizabeth and looked a lot nicer. There was a police SUV in the parking lot when we checked in, but it didn't matter.

Monica and I put the rooms in our names. Since Monica had a Michigan ID, it didn't look like we were all together, which made sense, I guess. If one of us got caught, the rest of us wouldn't have to go down too.

Monica insisted on getting the work room in her name. She said she had been there before, and that every room had a Jacuzzi and free porn. I didn't care about any of that, and unlike her, I wasn't in no rush to masturbate. That's all she talked about.

The room I got was a two-bedroom apartment. It was nice, too—no Jacuzzi, but a full kitchens, a nice leather furniture set, and free porn. Of course, Mama and Papa got the master bedroom, while Story and Marcos rushed for the other room, leaving me the option of joining them or sleeping on the couch. I took the couch.

First things first. I rushed into the bathroom to clean myself up. The bathroom was really nice and clean, too. I was impressed. Mama and Papa's master bedroom had a bathroom in it, so I didn't need to rush getting dressed.

As I waited for the tub to fill up with water, I stripped down naked. There was a full body mirror on the wall that I could use to get a good look at myself. I looked good, almost like I had matured five years since getting out of jail. My body was sexy—small but sexy. I couldn't weigh any more than a hundred pounds, but I looked good!

Once I sat back in the tub, finally relaxing a bit, the sound of a knock at the door made me lose control.

"What?" I yelled.

Without knocking again or answering me, Papa threw the door open. "Excuse me!" he said. "I thought you might want to hit this blunt."

I smiled. Actually, I was happy to see him. He closed the door behind himself and sat on the toilet next to me. I was laying there naked, but he wasn't paying me any attention. Most men would drool over the sight of a naked woman, but he wasn't like a normal guy. He was a pimp, which meant he saw naked women all the time. As crazy as it might sound, him not being thirsty or drooling at me made me feel more comfortable around him. He made me feel comfortable just being myself.

"I think I'm about to start my period soon," I told him, talking with the smoke from the piff in my mouth.

"That's okay. We will go after you get dressed and get some tampons and makeup pads. There is a Target up the road," he said, and then he whispered, "There is this Mexican restaurant called Chevy's in the plaza, they have margaritas for happy hour."

"That's all your ass do is drink margaritas," I joked.

"No it's not . . . I talk shit and swallow shit!"

"You do that!" I caught myself.

"Lean forward," he said and then he grabbed my towel and scrubbed my back. It was rough a little but really turned me on. He finished by rubbing the towel over my erect nipples.

After he left the bathroom, I was so turned on I had to bring myself to orgasm. All my life I had never experienced a man who made my body react the way he did. This man was special. Or was he just a pimp? Really, it didn't matter what he was. I'd had it rough my whole life, and now I felt in control for the first time.

There was some sense of happiness there. I knew that over the time I'd been on the road and in the game with him, I'd made a few thousand dollars. I could easily take off and make that money for myself, but I didn't want to. I liked being Papa's ho; it was like being Daddy's little girl in some sick way. Just knowing that I could always do this on my own was all the security I needed.

We all rode to Target together. At first, Papa made it seem like it was going to be just us two, but I should've known better than that. The few moments that we got to spend alone were always very short-lived.

Once we got to Chevy's restaurant, I was hungry. I ordered some sizzling steak fajitas, some corn tamales, and a frozen margarita. The food was delicious; even though the bill came out to $250, it was worth it. So far, from the gas, rooms, toiletries, and food, we had spent over a thousand dollars, and the day hadn't even started yet. Not for us, anyway. Monica stayed at the room, working.

Papa made sure he ordered Monica something to go, and he got her some things from the store, too. He took care of Monica differently than anybody else. She had a way of demanding respect by always working the most and going the hardest. It seemed like Papa had respect for her, too, kind of like having someone, if nobody else, that he could count on. They had been on these routes before, and he knew what to expect from her, so he gave her space.

Mama was totally different from anybody else. She was the only one who questioned Papa, and she hardly said anything to him in front of anybody else. They had a real relationship, and he loved her no matter what she did behind closed doors. I always wondered what went on between them two in private. I bet she knows his secrets, and I bet he makes love to her. The crazy thing about it was that there was no way for me to know, because they kept their relationship private. I do know that Mama was the glue to the game. There was no way I would still be around if it wasn't for her.

When we got back up to the hotel, there were police cars everywhere. Papa almost lost his mind. He called and called Monica, but she didn't answer. He was worried something was wrong.

He told everybody else to go to the room, and me and him walked around to the bar upstairs by Monica's room. There were no police by her room, but she wasn't answering her phone.

Papa took her spare room key, and we walked into her room. This bitch was naked and spread across the bed with the porn channel blasting. She had masturbated until she couldn't take it anymore and passed out, but the craziest part was that she had naked pictures of Papa on the screensaver of her phone. There was some money on the nightstand, I didn't know, maybe about four hundred dollars, which was good considering that she had made all that within a couple of hours.

"Get your nasty ass up and answer them text messages," Papa said so loud it made her jump.

"I wasn't asleep!" She jumped up real fast but then fell back down from the head rush. She then noticed Papa had brought her some food.

"Thank you, Daddy!" she said, finally getting up and exposing her naked body to us both. I'd never had a good look at her body before. She had a small baby pouch and some decent-size breasts. She was tall as hell and slightly hunchbacked. I guess she was pretty—I mean, she had long blonde hair, pretty blue eyes, and a swag about herself. She was very ladylike, and a nympho. She had sex appeal.

"What's been going on so far?" he asked her. I sat down at the table trying to avoid watching the porn that was playing on the television. Papa noticed my discomfort and changed the channel to ESPN, which wasn't much better.

"I got a few addresses for tonight," Monica said. "Most of them are in the Edison and Woodbridge area. I set them up for after rush-hour traffic dies down."

"Good. I am going to leave her with you and Marcos for the night," he said, pointing to me. "Besides, you need some company to help you stay awake!"

"I don't need no fucking babysitter or to be babysitting anybody!"

Papa grabbed her by her hair, but not really hard, just to let her know he was serious. "Help her with her phone, because she will be covering her own calls, and I want you to set up all of yours and her calls at the Ranita Center Holiday Inn, if you get called down that way; but if they can't come that far, send them here. Story and Mama will be using this work room.

"I always get sent off," she mumbled. Then she said, "Well, can I at least go get a drink out of the bar after I get dressed?"

"One!"

Papa picked up the money except for forty dollars—or, should I say, two twenty-dollar bills—and then left. Soon as he left, Monica pulled her tight slutty dress over her head and we went over to the bar.

The bar was nice. It was upstairs on the second floor, with a nice leather couch and a few videos games in it. There were flat-screen televisions on the walls and one really large flat-screen in front of the couches. ESPN was playing.

"Want the same thing?" this redhead mixed bartender asked Monica. Then she looked me up and down before asking me if I wanted anything.

"Yes, and she will have the same," Monica ordered for me.

Before we finished our second drink, Marcos joined us at the bar. We went from being distant on the couches to now being at the bar enjoying ourselves with the patrons and business travelers.

My phone started ringing, and Monica's never stopped. By the time we left, we both were tipsy and had about ten dates apiece to do, both in—and out-calls.

I had been answering my own phone and had heard the script enough times to be able to catch on to it right away. Almost every call that I got, I closed. It was similar to telemarketing in a way. When I was locked up in the JJC girls' detention home, I had a job as a telemarketer at the Signature Guest, briefly. I was good at the calls but not at putting up with the supervisor, so I got fired after I got my first check.

"When we leave, grab everything," Monica told me. "We most likely won't be back to this room tonight."

"Okay!" I said, confused. "Where will we be?"

"If we get calls down in Edison, it's better for us to stay down in that area. Edison is about forty-five minutes from here in traffic and about thirty minutes off the turnpike, so better to relocate," she explained. "Besides, in the morning, he rarely stays in the same spot for more than one or two nights."

"How is he going to come get us if we in the van with Marcos?" I asked. My concern wasn't that we were getting sent off. What worried me was getting left someplace far away from Papa. It was one thing having everybody together, but to get sent away from the pack was another.

"Girl, relax. He won't leave us nowhere stranded, besides we going to have his money. I've been out here several times, and it's cool. Just relax and stay focused."

I listened to her. Really, I wasn't even worried, just cautious. All I knew was that I was far away from home selling my ass for this dude. I was on my period and cramping really bad. Now after I got done selling my bloody ass for this man, I got to wait to pay him. It just wasn't right.

The night went smooth. I did six dates. Most of my in-calls, which is where the tricks come to me, were for two hundred; the out-calls, where we drove to them, they gave me two hundred and fifty.

The makeup pads worked, too. They were actually amazing. I was thinking the tricks would know I had the thing lodged inside of me, but none of them did, and I didn't bleed on anybody.

The tricks in Jersey loved me! Most of them were Indians or Arabs. Not one nigga called my phone for dates; the ones who did were pimps trying to get me to choose up. I swear I had gotten so many text messages and dick shots from pimps it took up half my calls. Every time, I would text the pimps Papa's phone number. Papa said it's how he meets up with pimps around the world.

CHAPTER 12

The next day, I was awakened by the bright a.m. sun beaming into the room through the cracks in the heavy closed curtains. Other than the few strands of light gleaming in, it was dark in the room. I was asleep in one of the double beds with Monica. At first I didn't see any reason why we should share a bed, until we both had done several dates on the other one, and one of my dates was with this weird-ass guy who was embarrassed about his size. He was just a freak, but he wanted to get under the covers with me. Tricks were weird. They all wanted something different, but for the most part they were easy to please.

The hardest date I'd done so far was with this older white guy who was high as hell on cocaine. This dude wouldn't get hard, and on top of that he forced me to suck his soft dick for pretty much the whole hour. It was gross. He tipped me good, but still, I worked my ass off for that money.

The highlight of the night was Papa texting to check with me the whole night. He was so sweet to me, even promised me a surprise, which I really wasn't concerned about. I had fun just talking back and forth with him. I even sent him a hot naked picture of me with my legs spread open. He loved that! At least, that's what he said.

Marcos was sweet too, although Monica rode in the front seat the whole night. He wouldn't smoke the piff up without me while I was gone on my dates; he made sure I had condoms and KY Jelly every time before I got out of the van. He even offered me some of his chicken nuggets.

Something was different with him when he was around Papa and when he was the only man around. He really stood up and showed me a different side when he offered to help me take my bags up to the room. I was getting my sunflower seeds, charger, and the rest of my things out of the back of the van when I found another open Magnum rapper. At first

I thought I was crazy—I could've been tripping—but finding yet another condom was too much of a coincidence. I picked it up and put it in my pocket.

"You up?" Monica asked me, still laying down facing the window.

"Yes," I said, breaking from my trance.

"We need to get dressed, because we have to catch a cab to the train station and catch the train up to Linden," she said.

"Why?"

"I guess that's what Daddy wants us to do, because something happened to the van and it's in the shop at Pep Boys."

"I knew this shit was going to happen," I said, jumping up. I was pissed and scared. I had never been on a train before and felt abandoned. I lit up a Newport.

Monica ignored me. She was the first one up, so I let her jump into the shower first. I wasn't surprised when she put the same dress back on.

I got dolled all up in another pair of leggings and some purple sandals with a purple blouse to match. My wardrobe was growing fast. I already had almost a different outfit for every day of the week. Honestly, that was more clothes than I'd had my whole life.

While we waited on the cab to take us to the train station, we ate at a restaurant, Famous Harold's, in the hotel lobby. It was good but weird. They sold pounds of sliced deli meat and loaves of bread for two to eight people. It was quiet expensive, and to top it off, they had this pickle bar, which let me tell you, was very delicious. Growing up with my mother, I used to love when she came home from the store and always brought my sister and I these spicy pickles. That was so long ago; it's crazy how me sitting here in New Jersey, at a pickle bar, takes me back to those times.

Our cab driver was Indian, and he barely spoke English. He wore one of those scarves wrapped around his head like you would see in a movie. The car smelled musty and heavy, and the foreign music was playing loud. It just about drove me crazy. He was driving extremely fast, like he was in a rush to go somewhere. The driver was an asshole, too; he dropped us off on the wrong side of the tracks on purpose, meaning we had to walk all the way around to the other side of the tracks to catch the train going north. There were at least fifty other people out waiting for the train. Monica and I stood out the most, but everybody seemed too stuck in their own lives to care what we were doing or where we were going, looking like hookers—at least Monica did!

"Give me your money from last night," Monica demanded as soon as we sat down on the train. I had my Sony earplugs in my left ear listening to a Pandora radio station, but I left the other one out just in case she said anything important.

"For what?" I snapped back, taking out the earphones.

"Look, I made more money than you anyway, but that doesn't matter. He will be more happy if we hand him our money in one bankroll than separate. Trust me! I don't want credit for your hard work."

I hesitated. My first thought was that she was either trying to steal money out of her money and then use my money as a cover up, or that she was being nosy and all up in my business. Then I decided, *What the hell.* I gave her my money without counting it and put my earplugs back in.

The train ride was smooth. I was able to relax with my eyes closed. Monica was playing some dumb game on her phone the whole time. My phone was much nicer than hers, so I didn't play with it in her face.

Once we finally got to our stop and got off the train, Papa was the first person we saw. He was up on the north ramp by himself, dressed up in an outfit I hadn't seen before, which must of meant they went shopping.

"You went to the mall without me?" Monica yelled like a crying baby who didn't get her way in public, causing a scene.

The same people we saw on the train all stood shaking their heads at us in disgust. It's weird, too, because the attention we were getting made me feel proud to be a whore. Who cared what people thought? Only person that mattered to me was Papa.

Papa whispered sternly, "Bitch, what the fuck is you waiting for?" He had his hand out.

My heart dropped. I didn't know what to do. In an instant, I went from being proud to ashamed. Only thing I didn't want was for him to slap her or me in front of the crowd. Something told me he would do it, and on top of that, I still didn't know why.

Monica understood what was going on, and instead of just paying Papa, she made him wait. Now I knew why she wanted my money so bad—because I would've handed over my bankroll proudly!

"Oh, here!" she said, acting like she forgot. It pissed me off more because she handed it all to him like it was from her and never even said anything about what I did.

Papa looked at me, then at her, and after shoving the money into his pocket, he said, "Well, since your funky ass seem to done forgot to pay a pimp, I guess I need to teach you."

"What is that supposed to mean?" she asked, scared, but it was too late. He had already walked off to the kiosk machine and was putting money inside.

"Daddy, I don't want to go home. I was going to give you your money!"

He ignored her and let her just embarrass us all in front of the crowd of strangers. I stood my distant ground. There was no place for me between them. Even though my money was inside that money, I wasn't the one who hesitated. I put my earplugs back into my phone and cut my Pandora radio back on. Wherever we were heading, didn't matter to me. I just followed them back onto the train and sat in the seat behind them.

Honestly, I was pissed off and really wasn't up for games. I had been ignoring my brother's text messages and my mother's phone calls. What was I supposed to tell them? Here I was on a train for the second time in my life on the same day, and from the looks of things, I was heading to New York City.

Papa threatened to send Monica home, but he hadn't said anything to me or about me leaving. I really didn't care if I left or not. Leaving didn't scare me as much as what might happen if I stayed.

"You want to go or stay?" Papa asked me after nudging my arm to wake me up. I must have dozed off or something, because when I looked up, he was sitting next to me and Monica was alone in her seat looking out of her window, still crying.

"What do you want? I am here with you?" I said nervously.

"I want you to stay," he told me, looking me in the eyes. "But I understand if you want to go home and see your son."

Him speaking of Carlton made tears form instantly in my eyes. As much as I tried to hold them in, I couldn't. "Carlton?"

"Excuse me?"

"Carlton. It's my son's name!" I yelled.

Still looking me in my eyes, he said, "Listen here, bitch, I want you to get something clear, right here, right now. I don't give two fucks what your son's name is. I don't give a fuck if you ever see him again. All I give a fuck about is the next date your little worthless ass do and if you get a tip or not. So next time you feel the need to correct me about your little bastard's name, make sure the trick that buys you from me and gets you pregnant is a millionaire!"

After the first few words came out of his mouth, I blanked out. All I saw was his lips moving, but the words that followed weren't as important. I knew Monica heard him too, and I knew that was his intention.

I spit directly into his face. I did it for me, I did it for Monica, but most of all, I did it for Carlton. Then I jumped up and tried to get out of my seat, but he grabbed my wrist and jerked me back down.

Sitting down, I looked around the train for help. To my surprise, not one person even paid us any attention. I sat there with my heart jumping up out of my chest. Monica acted like she wasn't paying us any attention, but I felt her presence. She was loving every minute of it.

"I want to go home!"

"Good for you. Hope you got some money saved up inside that bloody pussy of yours, because that's your only hope," he whispered coldly.

"No, you're fucking sending me home!"

The train stopped at the Secaucus Station. I was tempted to jump out and make a run for it, but I didn't have any clue where Secaucus was. All I knew was that the next stop was Penn Station in New York City. I had seen enough movies to know that I had a better chance of getting home from there.

I pulled my phone out of my pocket and then, unexpectedly, the empty Magnum wrapper fell out of my pocket onto his lap. He looked down at it and then up into my eyes. The look he gave me was a betrayed look, but a moment later, fire crossed his eyes. It sent a shiver through my body. No words in the dictionary can describe the amount of fear I felt in my heart. My eyes were locked into his. He kept his eyes on me but reached up, causing me to flinch just enough for him to be able to snatch my phone out of my hand.

Instantly, I jumped for it, but I was not ready for the backhand that came across my face. I fell back into my seat.

"Hey!" this gray-headed older white guy yelled at us. "You are not going to sit here and abuse this young lady here on this train! Not with me on it!"

"What the fuck you going to do?" Papa asked, jumping up and standing face to face with the old man.

"It's okay," I said, reaching to pull Papa back to the seat.

"Get your fucking hands off me!" he said while pushing me back to my seat.

That was it. The old man gave a fierce right hook that sent Papa falling back on top of me. I tried to hold him down on top of me, because I knew Papa was capable of beating the old man up, and deep down inside, I wanted Papa to take the punch like a man. I felt he deserved it. That old man revenged me.

Not quite done with the first punch, the old man used Papa's disadvantage as a reason to reach over and grab him by the neck and start choking him so hard that the only thing Papa could do was grab the man's arms, trying to free his neck. He was gagging loudly, and they both were on top of me, squeezing me up against the window.

"Help! Get off of him!" Monica yelled, hitting the old man on the top of his head, catching him off guard.

The train finally came to a stop at Penn Station, with us all still fighting. The old man, tired of Monica hitting him on the head, finally reacted by releasing Papa's neck just in time not to kill him. Then he swung a wild swing, connecting with Monica in the face and causing her to fall down off the seat and into the aisle.

"I'm sorry!" the man said, going straight to helping Monica up off the ground. "I am so sorry, please let me make it up to you."

Papa, still gasping for air, said, "You almost killed me."

The police were on the scene instantly, with guns drawn on the old man.

"Down!" one of the officers yelled.

Still choking, Papa said, "It's okay."

"Sir. Please step back. This man is a threat!"

"It's okay. He meant us no harm," he said again.

"Ma'am," the officer asked Monica.

"It's fine," she said, getting up off of the ground. Her dress had pulled up, exposing her naked body from the waist down.

Everybody looked: the old man, the officer, and me. Papa grabbed her by the hand and then me, and we walked off.

"Wait!" the older man yelled to us.

We all stopped for a look around at the crowd. Papa's, Monica's, and my clothes were all over us, and we were all bleeding somewhere.

"What?" Papa asked, still holding both our hands.

"Let me make it up to you all. I at least owe you a drink," he said with his hand reached out.

Papa released my hand for a second and gave the man a firm handshake. It was cute. Deep down, I don't think Papa was ever going to fight the old man back in the first place. Besides, he maybe would've lost if he did. We all walked out of Penn Station together. The first sight of New York City was breathtaking. There were long lines of cabs and people waiting to catch one. There was a Borders Bookstore on the corner and a line of restaurants across the one-way street on 7th Avenue.

"Where you guys crashing at?" the old man asked. "By the way, Billy Sparrow."

"They call me Indiana," Papa said, not giving up his name. "This is Kassie and Monica."

"Nice to meet you, lovely ladies."

"We don't have a place yet. Kind of a spur-of-the-moment trip, if you know what I mean," Papa winked.

"I get it. Let's go over to the Affinia, over there. It's a nice place. I'll set you guys up."

"That's not necessary," Papa insisted.

"It's the least I can do. I have never done anything like that before. I feel horrible," he admitted. "I could be on my way to the nearest precinct."

Without another word, we walked across to the Affinia Millennium. It was on 7th Avenue and 32nd Street. I melted when we walked inside the hotel. It was like a hotel you see in the movies. There were doormen who let us in through the revolving doors that led us up to a huge staircase. Overhead there hung a crystal chandelier that made the burgundy plush carpet seem clean and not as worn out as it was. The lobby was adjacent to a bar that could only be reached through the hotel lobby; it was for the patrons who either stayed at the hotel or lived close enough to know of it, but it wasn't open to the public.

"Hey, Billy!" the bartender yelled over the disco music. There were about twelve stools unattended, waiting for us or other people who simply came to grab a drink or two and then leave. The place was blue and glass, with blue lights around the bar that made all the glasses seem blue.

"Hey, mate!" Gimme a few Jager bombs!" Billy yelled to him while at the same time grabbing Monica by the arm to escort her to a seat next to him. The bartender paid us no attention and never asked us for identification. He seemed to know Billy well.

I said nothing to Papa, and although he still seemed upset, he played along too. Maybe he was trying to figure out how we were going to get away from this old man, or maybe he was trying to figure out how to get rid of us all. He sat next to me, and I sat next to Monica, with Billy on the far side.

We all drank our drinks. They were gross, like licorice candy mixed with Red Bull. They went down smooth with a nasty aftertaste. The first one made me shiver and sent a chill down my spine, but it was followed by a second and then a third. By the time the third one went down, I forgot where I was. Monica and Billy took off to get a room. Papa and I were alone for the third time since I met him.

"I am sorry about earlier," he said to me. I was so tipsy that his words went in one ear and out the other.

"Sorry for what?"

"I don't want you to leave me. I guess I took everything out on you, and you don't deserve that," he said.

"You were mean to me, but I understand you have to be that way," I said, making up an excuse for him. He needed one.

"Not really. I don't have to be mean. I guess it's the fact that I feel like such a bad father to my own children that I put up this brick wall toward everybody else's. Of course I don't really feel that way about Carlton," he said clearly, to make sure I didn't get offended. "I want to apologize about that, okay?"

Instead of answering, I reached out and touched his hand. At first his hand clutched as if he wanted to jerk away, but then he relaxed and took my hand in his. It was a very intimate moment. The drinks were working a number on not just me but him too. He seemed sad!

The bartender came with another round and then slid the bill into one of the blue glass cups along the edge of the bar. He looked at us, realizing we had both reached the legal limit a few drinks ago.

I lit up a cigarette out of the same pack I'd had for almost two weeks. That cigarette was the last thing I remember from that night.

CHAPTER 13

I woke up on the bathroom floor, next to the toilet, naked. As much as I wanted to jump up and find out where I was, I couldn't move. The cool marble floor made the small but elegant bathroom feel like I was laying before heaven's gates, ready to enter.

First thing I noticed was that I had a towel wrapped around my waist in the attempt to cover me up, which failed because my shaved pussy sat out with a little spot of blood on the white towel. I was pretty much off my period, but didn't have a tampon inside me or a panty liner on. Had I had sex or not? I didn't know.

Barely able to stand up, I made my way out of my palace into the dark hotel room. The change from bright and all white to the dark room made me hesitate so my eyes could adjust to the room. I didn't know what to expect, so when I saw Mama laying across the bed with nothing on, I was a little disappointed. Where was Papa?

Instead of waking her up, and hoping to catch Papa naked, I made my way into the adjoining room. I found Story and Marcos asleep on the fold-out couch. Then I realized that Monica and Papa were gone together. I felt a surge of jealously but held it inside.

I looked at my clock and noticed it was close to four in the morning. There was no reason for me to lay back down. There was enough of that going on in the room, so I tiptoed back into the room with Mama and slid my dirty clothes back on. My clothes smelled like liquor and smoke. My phone was on the ground. Picking it up, I noticed several missed messages and texts from my brother and the dude from Chicago. He seemed to make it his business to say goodnight to me every night.

After I got my things, I snuck out of the room and then made sure to remember the room number. I was shocked—I had no clue how I had made it up to the eighteenth floor without remembering a thing. Was I slipped on?

The lobby wasn't how I remembered it either. It was no longer bright and colorful; now, it was dim, with the carpet exposing the water leaks that stained the floor. The doorman was running a vacuum over the sitting area. He didn't even look up at me. I opened the door myself.

Outside, the traffic had died down a lot, but it was still more traffic than I had ever seen before at this hour. There was a street sweeper sweeping along the side of the one-way street that I stood on, and the garbagemen led the way, picking up and tossing in the garbage that lined both sides of the street.

I didn't know which way was right or which way was wrong. All I knew was that, either way I went, I was in the middle of nowhere. I still had the twenty dollars I kept from the money I had, but I knew that twenty wasn't enough to get me anywhere. I also knew that of all the places in the world I could go, back upstairs to the room was the only place I didn't want to be.

I started walking to the right. It was cold. First thing I saw was a McDonald's that appeared out of nowhere. It was hidden inside the walls, like an office space. I was from a place where you found McDonald's by following the huge golden arches that painted the sky, but here in New York City the sign was so small I could've missed it. Only reason I noticed it was there was a line inside waiting to be served.

I stepped inside and noticed that the sitting area was upstairs and was closed. Before I turned to leave, a younger white guy asked me a question. I didn't hear him or care what he said. All I wanted was to hurry up and get nowhere fast!

"Excuse me?" he yelled coming out to chase me. "You dropped this."

I stopped and looked back. He was breaking his neck to hand me the twenty-dollar bill I had dropped. He wore a black cap, a dark brown long-sleeve button-up shirt, and some slacks that looked as if they cost a few hundred bucks. "Thank you," I said.

"No problem," he replied in a cool East Coast accent. "Sam."

"Kassie." I gave his waiting hand a light shake.

"Who was that gentleman you were at the bar with earlier?" he asked, catching me off guard.

"That guy? Excuse me? Do I know you?"

"No, no, no!" He used his hands to show me he wasn't trying to cause me any harm. "I am not a cop. Just was at the bar earlier and noticed you, that's all. I am staying at the Affinia over there."

"I don't remember you from the bar." I smiled, relaxing a little bit. "I was so trashed by the time I left there, I can hardly remember anything. I woke up on the bathroom floor of the room."

"Don't feel bad. I left there and went over to this bar called Roof Top on 34th Street and 8th Avenue and drank more shots. I had to grab a bite to eat before going in for the night."

"So, where are you from?" I asked, realizing that he was flirting with me. Maybe not really flirting, but opening up.

"I am from Wilmington, Delaware," he said, walking next to me back toward the hotel room. He had two sandwiches in his bag and handed me one.

"I am okay, thank you!" I insisted, trying to give it back.

"No, lady. You need it more than me. I am telling you, McChickens are the best thing for hangovers."

"I like my McChickens with ketchup, quarter-sliced onions, mustard, and pickles," I told him, almost embarrassed as soon as the words came out of my mouth.

He stopped. Then he took the sandwich out of my hand and went inside McDonald's and got everything I wanted added on it.

While he was inside, I waited out front for what seemed like forever. He was on his cell phone arguing visibly with someone. I wanted to walk off but I couldn't. I didn't know where to go if I did anyway.

A taxicab pulled up on one side of me, almost parking on the curb. As soon as I realized that the taxi wasn't a yellow NYC taxi but undercover police, I got scared.

"Don't move!" a hulking Latino officer yelled, drawing a gun on me.

Then two more undercover NYC cabs pulled up as well. I felt like I was on a movie set and it was all part of a scene. "What's wrong?"

"Don't move!" the Latino officer yelled again, this time scaring me to tears.

I sat there without moving, crying. There was nothing I could say or do. I had no clue what I had done so far anyway.

"Officer, is there something wrong?" Sam asked, coming out of McDonald's with what looked like more food than before.

"Don't move!" the Latino officer yelled. "There was a complaint about you and this hooker exchanging money out here on the street."

"Officer, that was a misunderstanding!" Sam laughed. "She dropped twenty dollars inside McDonald's, and I returned it to her. Come on! You must be kidding."

"Tell it to the judge!"

"Sir, this is a very huge mistake. I work for Clug. I am not a push-around," Sam yelled, pissed off.

"You make that kind of money and can only afford a twenty-dollar hooker?" the Latino officer joked.

"That's fucking enough. I am not going to sit here and let you call me a hooker. Fuck off!" I said, spitting in his direction.

The officer looked to his other officers, and they all shrugged their shoulders. "No hooker is dumb enough to spit on an officer. I could detain your little nasty ass and make you take a HIV test before releasing you!"

"Look, don't you have some crime to attend to?" Sam asked in a much calmer tone.

Without another word, the officer jumped back into his cab and smashed off down the avenue, followed by the other officer.

Sam stood his ground before he approached me. Maybe he let the hooker talk bring him to reality, maybe not. He handed me a bag with two freshly made McChickens, and then he grabbed my arm and escorted me back to the hotel.

On my way back toward the room, several thoughts crossed my mind. The first was that Sam was a nice-looking guy who had just stood up for me in front of the law, and the next was that going back inside that hotel was the last thing I wanted to do.

Deep down inside, I wanted to tell Sam that I was a prostitute and wanted three hundred dollars for the hour, but for some reason, after the way the police had just treated me, I couldn't come to grips with the idea. Not to mention that, for some odd reason, I felt in my heart obligated to hand the money over to Papa.

I stopped in mid-stride, causing Sam to stumble over himself to catch his balance.

"I . . ." I couldn't get the right words out of my mouth. The sun was peeking through the early dawn clouds, hidden behind the skyscrapers that formed the backdrop of the picturesque scene.

"What's wrong?" Sam asked, seeing the concern in my eyes. Being a lady, I could always tell a horny man who wanted between my legs. Sam was different; he was more of a protection, more of an established man than I was used to being around. "Did I do something?"

I let his arm loose from mine. The early morning commuters were filling the once-empty streets. Horns were blowing, and the trash that had filled the streets was gone as if it never existed. "I'm not ready to go back to the room yet. I mean . . ." I hesitated again.

"Are you okay?" he asked me.

"Yes, I'm fine," I lied. "I am just kind of trying to breathe, you know?"

He did. He gave me a look that not only melted my heart but also made a lovely tear roll down my face. I didn't want to cry, especially in front of this stranger, but I couldn't control the tears. They were from so deep down inside my heart that I would need a map to find them again.

"Come here," he said, reaching out to me and wrapping his arms around me.

I let him embrace me but didn't hug him back. Instead, I laid my head on his muscled chest and began to cry uncontrollably. "I don't know what's wrong with me!"

"It's okay!"

"It's not okay!" I screamed into his chest.

"Well, what can I do to help?"

"Just do like the rest of the world and act like I don't exist. Ignore me. Fuck me! Beat me!"

He pushed me away from his chest without letting go of my arms, but far enough to force me to make eye contact. "I don't want to leave you out here for the police to mess with you. At least let me take you somewhere. I was at the New Yorker over there on 8th Avenue across from the Roof Top Bar last night. Let me put you in a room so you can be alone for the night and then tomorrow, I would like to take you out somewhere nice."

That gesture made me smile. He smiled too. Then he took one of the napkins out of the McDonald's sack in his hand and wiped my eyes dry.

It was so sweet. The smell of the food from the bag covered my face and reminded me how hungry I was. I took his hand in mine and used my free hand to take one of his sandwiches from out of his bag, open it, and then offer him a bite. He took it and then gestured with a nod of his head for me to do the same. I took a bite too, and as much as I hated the taste of mayo and lettuce, that bite was the best bite I could ever remember having in my life.

The walk over to the New Yorker wasn't as far as I thought. We walked past Madison Square Garden and then were on 33rd and 8th Avenue. We hadn't said a word to each other, but I felt Sam's mind wandering—maybe onto sex, maybe onto the taxi police who were circling the block looking at us, but he kept his cool.

"Do you want to come with me?"

"No," he replied. "You need to be alone. Here is my card. Just text me when you get up."

"But I wanted you to join me," I said, and I did.

"If you still want me to join you tomorrow, then we will make it a date," he said. "Look, uummm . . ."

"Kassie."

"Well, Kassie," he smiled. "I know what you do. I don't want to judge you or anything like that, so let me give you this."

I looked down, and as he stuffed some bills into my pocket, I gave him a peck on the cheek and headed through the lobby to the elevators. The lobby wasn't nearly as big as the Affinia, but it was just as nice. There was a man in the elevator who pushed the PH on my request.

"Penthouse, huh, lovely lady?" he smirked. "Must be nice."

I didn't even know what that meant except for the fact that my floor was on the top of the list. Once I exited the elevator, it seemed like I was on a different level of life. There were four rooms, all with glass doorways. I slid my key in and opened up the door to heaven. The curtains opened up automatically, the lights from the skyline view of New York City made my heart sing, and the sun peeking over the horizon was the most beautiful thing I'd seen in my life.

I took my phone out and took a picture of the scene and then added it to my pictures to send a message to Sam. "Thank you."

"You like it?" he replied.

"I love it!"

"You deserve so much more," he sent with a smiley face. "Tomorrow?"

"Can't wait!" I admitted.

After I got done texting him, I filled up the Jacuzzi. My clothes fell off of my body instantly, followed by me jumping into the old-fashioned tub. A moment or so later, room service arrived.

"Come in!" I yelled, using the bubbles to cover my body.

The lady entered and poured me some champagne with orange juice and a strawberry on the rim of the glass. She placed a plate of strawberries next to the bottle with a pint of freshly squeezed orange juice.

"If you need anything else, here's the menu. Don't worry about a thing, it's going to be billed to the room," she said in her broken English.

"I appreciate it!"

After she left, I received a text message from Papa with just a question mark. My heart dropped! I texted him back a question mark.

"Call me!" he said.

"Hi," I said, afraid for my life. The sound of his voice scared me but made me feel safe all at the same time.

"You okay?" he asked. I could tell he was pissed but wouldn't show it.

"I'm fine."

"Where are you?"

"I'm at the New Yorker," I admitted.

"You on a date?"

"Not really!" I said. "I got a room!"

"I will be there in a minute!" he said and hung up.

I texted him the room number and then relaxed for the little time I had. My mind was telling me that Papa and the crew would be here momentarily to mess up my vibe. Crazy part about it was that I didn't mind. The few breaths of fresh air I'd had were all I needed.

Chapter 14

The sound of the phone ringing next to my head woke me. I looked up at the sky through the window and was blinded by the glare from the sun.

I answered the phone. "Hello?"

"Are you expecting a visitor, Ms. Kassie?" the greeter asked. "A gentleman that says he is your brother?"

Caught off guard, I remembered Papa was on his way. "Yes, send him on up."

I looked over to the time on my phone, and it was nine in the morning. I was still inside the water, and the feeling of it soaking inside my skin made me feel like a new person.

I jumped out and went to crack the glass door. I wrapped myself up in the robe that hung on the doorway. Then Papa entered.

"Hey!" I said. I shivered. The look in his eyes sent a chill through me. I went straight for my clothes and pulled out the money Sam stuffed inside my pockets. "I haven't counted it."

Papa didn't either. He spread the bills in his fingers and, once satisfied, stuffed the small wad into his pocket. The sound of paper bills stuffing his pockets like a stuffed animal was alarming.

He had come alone, which surprised me a bit. I used to want to be alone with him, but at times like this I wished Mama was there to protect me.

"I thought you left me!"

"I . . ."

"Shh!" he said with a finger to his lips. "This is a nice room!"

"Thank you!"

"The next time you leave without letting me know, I will leave you behind."

I ignored him and got myself another drink, making him one too, and also putting strawberries on the rim of the flute. "I was trying to make some money, and I did!"

Before I could get the words out good, Papa was up in my face in a flash. "Did I fucking send you to go make some money, bitch?"

"No!" I trembled. "But we . . ."

"But what?"

"I am sorry!" I flinched as he reached extra fast toward my face but stopped and took one of the drinks from my hand.

"Thank you," he said now in a sweet voice. Then he drank the drink like he was drinking Jager bombs the night before. I did the same.

"You thirsty?" he asked me. Then without another word, he sat at the edge of the bed and opened up his True Religion jeans. "You need to drink this pimp juice, not orange juice and champagne."

I smiled. Nothing I could say or do but follow suit. As much as I resisted in my heart, my body was under his control. I didn't feel like sucking his dick. I was tired of sucking dick. I wanted to be made love to.

Without complaining, and obligated like a wife to her husband, I was obligated to my pimp. I got on my knees and put his large dick in my mouth. The taste and smell of pussy on him made me gag, but I kept a smile on my face. After a few strokes on him, he was hard as a rock. He stood up and bent me over, lifting my robe up over my butt. I thought he was going to just ram inside of me, but instead he got down and ate my pussy from behind.

I was on my knees on the edge of the bed with him behind me, with his face buried in my pussy. He wasn't the best pussy eater I'd had, but God, the power, the control, all made me go so crazy that I came within the first minute. He kept going until I crawled away from his face. I couldn't take anymore. I was so sensitive, it made me uncomfortable.

Without losing his stride, he got up and grabbed my waist with both hands. He pulled me forcefully back to the edge of the bed and then slid his dick inside my pussy and straight to my head. First thought I had was of Story telling me how he was the best lover she had ever had. Next thought was of my son Carlton, and how Papa was inside of me unprotected. Then the feeling of him filling me up. There was a gush of warm juices flowing inside of me, followed by the grunting sound of Papa finishing up.

"That was great!" he moaned to me, laying back on the bed with his pants still down to his ankles.

"I thought so too!" I agreed. I'd had better, but I didn't care. Nothing was better than the last few minutes I had spent with Papa. I don't think I'd ever come so hard before in my life. I was confused.

I went to the bathroom and washed my pussy up and sat on the toilet to try to push the cum out of me. There was a lot coming out into the water, but I knew it didn't matter. If I was pregnant, I was pregnant, and being pregnant was the last thing I needed. After cleaning myself up, I took a warm, soapy towel and washed Papa up as well. He was asleep like a baby, and he didn't budge until the warm towel was followed by the breeze in the room. He pulled his pants up and then laid back on the bed with his arms out to me. I didn't know what to do.

I lay next to him, and he wrapped his arms around me. His arm seemed to cast a shadow over the entire room, causing the bright sun, loud horns, and sound of a whistle to drain out instantly.

That feeling was a first for me. All my life I'd dreamed of having a man of my own, one who would hold me in his arms the way this pimp I was laying next to did. A tear came to my eyes, but this time it was a tear of joy. I was happy! If only for this minute, I was happy. He squeezed me so tight that I felt like the key to a deadbolt lock. This feeling was worth all the names, all the harsh words, and all the money in the world.

What I wondered was, how he could make so many of us feel this way? I wondered if this was a shared feeling. Was he as good a lover to Mama, Monica, or Story? I thought that if it was anyone else who shared these arms with him the way I was at the moment, then she was just as lucky as me!

None of that mattered anymore. I laid there in silence for over an hour, not budging. The sound of his light snores, the smell of his day-old cologne and cigar breath, eased my mind, putting me into a state of meditation.

His phone vibrated constantly. I dared to reach for it to stop it and prayed it wouldn't wake him from my arms. I knew this moment would be short-lived, and so what? I cherished the moment while it lasted.

My phone vibrated on the glass table next to the tub, causing it to make a disturbing sound. If I didn't answer my phone, it would wake him anyway, so I tried to ease out from under Papa's grasp, but as soon as I pulled away a little, he squeezed me tighter. After fighting me for only a minute, he released me and rolled over away from me, turning his back to me as if I never existed. I went for my phone and then slipped into the bathroom so that I wouldn't wake him up. I had a bunch of text messages from my brother, Mama, and Story.

"What?" I asked my brother after he answered on the first ring. He had sent me a message in all caps, threatening me if I didn't call him back.

"What do you mean *what*?" he snapped. "You just up and disappeared. Don't you think I worry about where you're at? And I already heard what you're doing!"

"What the fuck is that suppose to mean?" I asked.

"It's all over Facebook, how you all out of town with Marco selling pussy!"

"That's none of your fucking business!"

"Is Marcos pimping you?" he asked.

"Hell no! Marcos ain't no pimp! Where are you getting this shit?"

"Marcos's girlfriend Lisa is having a Facebook war with him about you. I guess she think you and Marcos is fucking!"

"That's bullshit!"

"Tell that to Marcos. Look on his page. He got pictures of you all on his page and shit . . ."

My mind blanked. Why would Marcos have any pictures of me on his page, and who the fuck was this bitch Lisa? As I was talking to my brother, my phone buzzed in my ear.

"So, for the record. I am not out here with Marcos. I am with my friend Stacey. Marcos is a driver. He ain't no pimp!" I corrected him, but I never said I wasn't selling pussy. I think my brother knew better anyway.

"Oh, another thing. Jackie left a number for you to call her. She wants you to call her ASAP, and that little cute white girl Lindsay keeps calling my phone trying to get me to pick her up again."

"Again?" I asked.

"Well, I kind of did pick her up and take her over to the studio."

"Carlton?"

"What?"

"What did you do to her?" I asked.

"Whatever we did, she sure liked it. That girl wants me to come pick her up every day!"

"Leave her alone, please!" I begged.

"Call her. I think she ran away from home and don't got nowhere to go. She wants to go with you or some shit."

"Okay! I will call her, but I want you to take her to the bus station for me if she needs a ride, okay?"

"Only if you promise to keep in touch."

I was silent for a minute. "I promise," I finally replied.

I hung up the phone and went back into the room. Papa was now up but still laying down looking through his phone. His pants were on the bed, but he was under the covers.

"Count that for me," he said with a nod toward his pants. "How much did this guy give you?"

"I never counted it," I said, sitting on the edge of the bed and grabbing the wads of money out of his front and back pockets. There was so much money piled up on the bed I could've bought a nice house or car with it.

Papa didn't pay it no mind. I counted the money Sam gave me first. I knew what it was because my old twenty-dollar bill was the only bill that wasn't a hundred-dollar bill. He gave me seven hundred dollars. I put all the money in order. I put all the bills in order—all the bills in piles of their own. There were ninety-two hundred-dollar bills; I almost fainted. By the time I put all the twenties and fifties in stacks of their own, I counted $16,211. I was shocked! It all made sense, but I acted like I wasn't impressed. Mama taught me to never seem amazed.

After counting, I folded the money up in as many bundles as I could and then tried to stuff them back inside his pockets.

"I have to ask you something," I said.

"What?"

"I have a friend named Lindsay who wants me to send for her."

"What's wrong with that?"

"I don't know."

"How old is she?" he asked, looking me in the eyes.

"I think she is eighteen," I lied.

"Then cool!" he said, reaching out to me again. I let him pull me on top of him, and within a few seconds, his juices were flowing up inside of me like a river.

There were times when I felt as if I didn't exist among the other girls, but now I felt almost used up, maybe even a little taken advantage of. Just the day before, this man had spoken so cruelly about my son, and now here he was pumping me up with his so-called pimp juice. What would he do if I ended up pregnant by him? Even more importantly, how many other bitches was he also cumming inside of without any protection?

I called Jackie. "Hello!" she said on the first ring.

"Hi!" I screamed. All I could hear was the static sound of her screaming back into the phone at the same time as me.

"Kassie, what the hell is wrong with you?" Jackie asked me.

"Girl, you will never guess where I am at!" I told her excitedly. Papa looked at me twice and then at his pants on the bed stuffed with money. He grabbed them and made his way to the shower. I rolled my eyes at him and he smiled. I would have never stolen any money from his ass anyway.

"Kassie?" Jackie yelled, trying to get my attention.

"Yeah, girl! Like I was saying."

"Where are you?" she asked me impatiently.

"I am in New York City, girl!"

"I miss you! When are you going to come see me?"

"I don't know," I said. "Where are you?"

"Tampa Bay, Florida," she said in an excited way. "It's nice as hell here, and it's guys everywhere."

"Guys?" I asked protectively.

"Yeah, Kassie!" she snapped. "It's not like I am a baby. I am eighteen now."

"So what? I am still older than you, and you will always be my baby sister," I reminded her.

"Come see me then!"

"Okay, I will, but you got to give me some time."

"Okay, so this is your number?" she asked.

"Yes, call me anytime."

"I love you, Sis!" she said, making me melt inside.

"I love you more!" I said, which was how we always responded to *I love you* growing up.

After I got off the phone with my sister, I felt lonely. Those few minutes talking to her felt better than all the moments I'd spent on earth.

Papa came out of the shower naked. He was on the phone with someone, maybe Mama, because he was being sweet. He was only sweet when talking to her or Liz.

My phone vibrated, and it was a text message from Sam. I really didn't know how to deal with Sam. He had already gave me seven hundred dollars plus a room. Now he might expect some pussy for free.

"You up, sunshine?" he texted.

"Yes, handsome," I texted back.

"Who is it that has you smiling like that?" Papa asked me, sneaking up behind me and again wrapping his arms around me. All this affection was more than I had ever had all my life.

"This guy Sam, the one that paid for this room."

"This 'guy'?" he asked with his nose turned up to me. "You mean trick?"

"Well, he isn't actually a trick yet. I haven't fucked him or even told him that I was working."

"What the fuck you mean? What do he think you are then?"

"I mean," I hesitated, "he knows, I think."

"What are you saying?"

"Look, he kind of saved me last night when the police approached me. They were calling me a hooker and saying I was working."

"You are a hooker," he said so coldly that my heart sank. "He didn't save you . . . Only thing that he did for you was pay me, bitch. Don't you ever get that twisted."

"Sorry!"

"Don't be sorry! Last thing a pimp needs is a sorry bitch! Call that trick and not only tell him you're a whore, but *my* whore. Tell him that I am your pimp, and that if he don't come pay me my other $1,300 for last night, then I am going to drown your funky ass in this Jacuzzi and stick this bottle up your ass first," he laughed. He made himself a drink, took a sip, and then splashed the rest of it in my face. "Now get dressed! And tell housekeeping to clean up this place!"

"I hate you!" I yelled and then picked up the glass and tossed it at the door. It was too late. He was out of the door, and he didn't turn back.

I cried my heart out. I cried so long that I started laughing. This fool had some nerve. I went into the bathroom, and my same old worn-out twenty-dollar bill that Cathy gave me was on the toilet. What was this, a tip for a job well done? Heartless bastard!

CHAPTER 15

The next day, we were heading down the Garden State Parkway toward Atlantic City. Liz, Lindsay, me, and Mama were all riding in the back of the van, laying on the fold-out bed. Story and Monica were both asleep in the two backseat reclining chairs. Marcos was asleep too, and Papa was the one driving, with the music off. Every time he drove, he either rode for hours in silence or listened to Sade. The silence and soul music were both therapeutic and disturbing at the same time.

Lindsay had been talking the whole time since she got into the van at JFK. I knew this was going to be a mistake. She was so unaware of what it was she was about to do. Liz told her the basics about doing dates, but she didn't tell her of the harsh words, the cold streets, or that even though it was raining, we'd still have to work the track.

Mama, as usual, put Lindsay next to her. She didn't even give me a chance to teach her myself. In a way, I didn't appreciate being left out, but in a way I was glad Lindsay was learning from Mama and not me. That way, if she messed up, I wouldn't be held accountable.

"Kassie?" Lindsay yelled, disturbing the peace. I knew by the way she was sounding that she was about to ask me a stupid question.

"What?"

"Tell Mama about when we was locked up and I used to sneak over to the boys' side and get some dick!"

I was right. I didn't even look her way. I was watching the rearview mirror, catching Papa's cold stare. He was already pissed off because she had identification but was only seventeen until the end of the month. I never expected him to make such a huge deal out of it, but it pissed him off.

"That's old, girl," I said. "We need to focus on today. The past is the past."

Papa, having heard enough, turned on the Sade CD *No Ordinary Love*. I felt bad too. He was so sweet to me, except for the drink he threw in my face, which I needed, because what he had me tell Sam actually worked. He not only gave me $1,300, but another $2,000, so all and all he spent $4,000 on me for two nights, and I only slept with him once.

Sam was sweet, though. He took me walking to the theatre district to see *Jersey Shore*, the musical, which I loved because when I was locked up I never missed a show. Then he took me to Luigi's Pizza to share a cheese pizza, which I never thought would taste so good. I grew up eating Papa John's or Pizza Hut, maybe Saylor's Pizza, but I never saw those places around here. All I saw were food carts and hotdog stands. Other than that, he got me a sketch of us together and bought me a bootleg Coach bag. I had never been in public with a white man on my arm, but he held my hand the whole day.

"Daddy!" Liz yelled over the music. He instantly looked up in the rearview and smiled. She yelled, "I got to pee!"

Monica looked up from under her Mickey Mouse blanket dead into Liz's eyes and then rolled hers and put her head back under the covers and yelled, "And I need some cigarettes!"

"Shut your funky ass up, bitch!" Papa yelled.

Lindsay had been in the car over two hours now and had heard a few *funky bitches* already, but this one was different. If she knew or had learned the game like me, she would know that when he spoke to one, he spoke to all. Which meant that if he called one a funky bitch, he called the others that, and he treated four the same way he treated two.

If he's in love with you, it's even worse, because he may take advantage of you. Since he is Daddy and Stacey is Mama, if you kiss you just better not tell. Just like the mothers in the world who know their husband or boyfriend, anyone else better keep quiet. Shame on you, because we as little girls have been through it.

That's what makes this game so cold—the fact that the dates are dangerous, but all us hos are tough as rubbers, we can go on date after date without touching or feeling skin. That can get old and feel like we're using a toy. We are the safest girls around the world having sex. You get hurt more just out there fucking around for free. Raw sex and being held are the dreams hos have.

Last night after my date, Papa came back to the New Yorker and stayed the night holding me. It felt like when my daddy used to sneak on top of me—those years I forgot about, those feelings I had let go of so long ago. I loved him though. How? I even forgot how long it had been. All I knew was that this love, fear, and hate that I had in my heart for Papa was real; he was so inside my head. I'd been so many places so fast, I had no clue what to expect. I knew my job and loved doing it. He was amazing!

Also, last night, before I let Papa cum inside me time after time, it was the first time fucking me in my ass. I counted his money again, and he had $19,000 before I added the money from Sam. Papa said he was teaching me how to do Greek dates by fucking me in my ass. The crazy part about it was how good it felt. He said I would be able to make more money and that he thought since I took it so well, I could be a "Greek goddess" and make more than the pink-toes online.

I wasn't crazy. I knew why he was fucking me in the ass, and I would probably let him do anything to me he wanted to. The simple fact that he wanted me made me happy. Now I wondered if my friend Lindsay was next, or was it Liz's turn to lay up, or was it just me that he wanted? Either way, I'd already detached my pussy from my heart, so I couldn't care less about anything else but making the most money tonight.

"Econo Lodge?" Lindsay yelled, disappointed. Papa again looked back to me before jumping out of the van.

"Girl, stop talking so much," I finally snapped.

"I am just saying! If I wanted to get a room at the Econo, I could have stayed in South Bend on Lincoln Way."

"Relax! He's just getting a work room," Mama said in a very soft tone. "He always uses the Econo here because it's outdoors and easy for him to watch us out on the track."

"So where we staying at?" she asked Mama, looking around. "The Tropicana, right there?"

"Never stay in a casino that we may work in," Monica interrupted. "The police will bust us if we stay at the casino."

Papa jumped back into the van and then pulled down to the dead end of the street. We could see the boardwalk ahead, but we were parked at the Days Inn at the end of the street.

"Mama!" he said. "You and Monica go get two doubles!"

"Why do I always got to go? Go here! Go there! A bitch get tired of getting sent the fuck off!" Mama snapped.

"Bitch!" Papa yelled. "I would slap you all the way upstairs, but that would feel too good."

"I am just saying! Damn!"

He ignored her. We all did. I bet she was just as glad to get slapped as we were that she didn't. "And make sure they connected!" he yelled.

"We know, Papa," Mama said, smiling on the way out.

Soon as Mama and Monica got out of the van, Liz jumped up to the front and sat on Papa's lap. She couldn't wait. All of us just watched as she claimed her number-three spot. He kissed her on the lips in front of us, but I bet he wouldn't have done that if Mama was in the van. Why do we got to get disrespected?

Liz was whispering something into Papa's ear, and whatever it was, he agreed, because the entire time he was nodding his head to her. Then, once she was done, she came back to the back with us as if she had never moved.

Mama came back and gave us all copies of the room key. Monica just grabbed her bags, mad, and ran off upstairs.

"Look!" Papa said. "I want you all to stay here. Marcos and I will be staying at the Econo. Get dressed and call me from the Borgota."

"How we suppose to get there?" Mama asked.

"Take the jitney!"

"What about Lindsay?" Mama asked, concerned. "She's not old enough to be running around the casino."

"Liz and Lindsay can stay here with me once y'all leave," he said, giving Liz a mischievous look. I knew then that she had planned this the whole time. "They can work the track."

"The track?" Story jumped in. "Why I got to go to the casino? Why can't I work the track?"

"Blade to the Borgota, and bitch, I make the rules!"

"Umm-umm!" she said under her breath and then went out first to the rooms.

"Daddy?" Liz jumped in. "Can I get dressed at your room?"

"That's up to Mama," he said. Then he looked at Mama and asked, "Do you mind, or do you want to get dressed in my room?"

Mama blushed. Then she said, "I don't mind. You can go down there to get dressed. Just use your room key to come up to the room when you get done getting dressed, because the doors lock in the lobby."

"Thank you!" Liz told her. They had a close bond, I could tell. Either that, or Mama just didn't want to be taken advantage of the way I had been over the past couple nights. She knew better. So did I. I was straight.

The rooms were nothing extravagant like we had in New York City, but they both had a nice view, facing the Atlantic Ocean and the boardwalk. I stepped out onto the balcony with Story to smoke a cigarette. She seemed pissed off about everything, but for the first time I felt her pain. Marcos was away from her, and he was like her only friend. They had something going on; I didn't quite understand it, but I could tell.

"I am so sick of these pink-toes and this whole bullshit game," she told me without taking her eyes off the dark ocean. It was windy but had stopped raining. The boardwalk was lit up and down, but the distant darkness of the ocean had a few lights from the boats and yachts that painted the background like a perfect picture.

The smell of dead fish filled the air, along with the freshly landed seaweed that flowed in with the roaring current, making my first time seeing the ocean one to remember. The empty world beyond my sight was a mystery in itself.

"Story?" I asked, breaking our silence.

"What's up?" she exhaled.

"Isn't this special?"

"What? This game?"

"No, this whole thing," I said, slowing her down. "Isn't it a dream come true to get to go to New York City, to see the Atlantic Ocean, the boardwalk in Atlantic City?"

She didn't respond at first. Then, after a moment of silence, she said, "I guess you can call this special, but I think it would be more special if we shared it with someone we loved, like a husband."

"But don't we love Papa? Isn't he that special someone?" I asked her out loud, but I was talking to myself.

When she looked at me, she shook her head and then walked away. Maybe she saw the love in my heart, maybe not. Either way, she felt my pain, and I felt hers. I spent another few moments staring into the darkness thinking about Papa. He was the man I loved, and there was nothing anyone could tell me.

All I knew was that if tonight I could make more money than all of them, then maybe, just maybe, I could share this view next to him.

I didn't care about dick or money; all I cared about was sharing one of these moments with Papa.

"Kassie!" Lindsay yelled from the bathroom. I had heard that voice for so long when we were locked up that hearing her now, here with me in Atlantic City, reminded me of jail. Another reality check.

"What's up?" I asked, stepping into the bathroom. "You look cute!"

"Thank you!" she blushed. Mama was doing her makeup and had put her in one of her dresses the same way she had dressed me up. The only difference was that, honestly, Lindsay looked much better than I did. She wore her dress just like a queen and walked around in Mama's wraparound stilettos with such style and grace. I would think she was twenty-one years old.

"Look at this!" She showed me the fake ID Monica had given her as well, which could pass except for the fact that the girl in the picture had red hair and was thirty years old. It was better than hers, but not by much. Who cared? It had to work. It didn't take long for me to get dressed up either, because I had already soaked all morning in the Jacuzzi at the New Yorker. I still jumped in the shower, and then I put on some black leggings and some of the heels from Rainbow that I hadn't worn yet.

By the time I was dressed, Liz was back, and that bitch had on a smile from ear to ear. We all just rolled our eyes at her. She didn't care, either. She was just a little sweetheart, with grimy written all over her face.

"You ready?" Mama asked Lindsay.

"I guess," she said, looking at me and realizing for the first time that this was real, but she didn't hesitate. She grabbed her things, and off her and Mama went.

Liz couldn't care less. She and Monica both seemed pumped up, but Story was laying down on one of the beds not even dressed.

"Could you come on?" Monica yelled at her.

Story didn't respond.

Liz looked and me and said, "You ready?"

"Yeah."

"Well, we about to go . . . I will text you if we get a date," she told Monica.

"I am coming!" Story jumped up and ran to the bathroom with an attitude, cursing out pink-toes under her breath.

"Okay! I will text your phone once we get done. Don't go far!" Monica told us.

"We going to the boardwalk, but not far."

Then we were off. The first thing Liz told me was, "I like you!"

"Thank you!"

"Just listen to me. I don't do no playing around," she demanded.

I didn't say shit. Actions speak louder than words. She was cool, but I didn't need her bossing me around. Now I saw why she chose me to come with her—so she could be the boss bitch. I didn't blame her. Monica couldn't care less either; they were in competition, and neither one of them saw me as a threat. Only I knew I was the one he slept up in the night before.

Before long, Liz and I were walking up to the Caesars casino. It was a long way, and people of all walks of life strolled and rode buggies the whole way up. There were vendors selling T-shirts, sweatshirts, dresses, bags, and bathing suits along the way. It was getting late, so most of the shops along the walk were closed.

I enjoyed the walk; it was peaceful. Liz didn't say anything to me, but she spoke to just about everybody else. Most of the guys who were out there were black or with a lady, which didn't stop Liz. She was friendly and gave her number out to whoever was looking to have some fun. Me, on the other hand, I wanted to just get the night over with. It was cold, and I felt so out of place.

"We suppose to be getting on the jitney," I said.

"Girl, please!" Liz corrected me. "The jitney is on Pacific, right on the strip. There is just so much more money, if not more, on the boardwalk."

"You see them looking at us?" I asked her, nodding my head toward six foreign guys who were standing in the casino bar. They were all dressed in black suits.

"Yeah, that's security!" Liz warned me.

"What they going to say to us?"

"They the biggest pimps in Atlantic City," she told me. "They will get us to the money."

Then she was off alone to talk to one of them. I sat down at a slot machine, afraid to insert my only twenty-dollar bill inside. I waited for a few minutes, and then one of the guys walked up and put a ten-dollar bill into the machine and whistled to a waitress who appeared out of nowhere.

"What are you drinking?" he asked me. He was the size of a pro ballplayer, handsome though, with a crooked smile.

"Top Shelf Margarita."

He laughed and then placed my order. Liz disappeared out of sight. I didn't even know her phone number, but I knew she was coming back. I hoped. The security guard said nothing to me the whole time, just stood there watching me like a hawk.

First stroke on the slot machine, I hit three sevens and they were all red, white, and blue. I had won a hundred dollars. The guard smiled but still didn't say a word. I wondered how many girls a day he sat up with.

Then here came an older white man. He looked at me and then walked up close to the security guard and asked, "What machine is winning tonight?"

"Try this one!" He pointed to my machine. "This lovely young lady has been a good-luck charm."

The older white guy handed him a folded-up bill and then slipped me a card with a room key and his room number. Then he sat down at my machine and cashed out my hundred-dollar winning ticket.

Soon as it came out, the security guard snatched it so fast I thought he was crazy, and then he looked at me, winked, and handed it to me.

"This machine will be waiting," he said.

CHAPTER 16

The entire night pretty much went the same. Date after date met and waited for me at my same slot machine. The waitress kept my same order coming, and Michael, my handsome security guard/pimp, kept me busy.

One of the dates that I did gave me permission to use his room for business purposes, which actually came in handy. Liz and I had a double date with these two young black guys from Camden; they were cheap but sweet. That was the only time I saw Liz the whole night. Most of the dates I did gave me a hundred dollars, which didn't bother me. What bothered me was the fact that Michael made me suck his dick for free after all the cheap dates he hooked me up with. Between the slot machines eating my money up and tipping my waitress, I had only made a little over six hundred dollars by the end of the night.

Papa texted me from time to time throughout the night, but by the time I had finished working, he had stopped. It was eight a.m. when I made it back to the Days Inn. My feet were killing me, I was a little drunk, and I was hungry as hell. The smell of the Country Kitchen in the hotel lobby got my stomach's attention. Instead of going upstairs to the room, I treated myself to some country biscuits and gravy. The food made me even more sleepy, but for some reason, I dreaded going up to the room.

Finally I went back, and to my surprise, Marcos and Story were the only people in the room. The adjoining room was empty, with the balcony door wide open. I stepped outside to smoke a cigarette and nearly pooped my pants when I saw Mama sitting down on the ground with tears causing her mascara to run down her face.

"What's wrong?" I asked, sitting down next to her, wrapping my arms around her the way she did me before.

"Papa got mad at me because he got drunk and lost all his money playing poker," she said. "I told him to stop while he was ahead!"

My head spun around. If Papa had lost all of his money, he had lost a lot of money. "How much did he lose?"

"I don't know." she sniffed. "A lot!"

"What's a lot?"

"Thousands!" she yelled. "Maybe two or three."

"That's not bad," I said, relieved.

"I know, but he was pissed off at me and so drunk that they put us out of the casino."

"Where is everybody?" I asked.

"I don't know. Nobody knows where Lindsay is, and Monica had an all-nighter with this UFC fighter, so she is still working. I am sick of this shit. We should have never come here."

"Lindsay is missing?" I asked. "Where is Liz?"

Mama looked me in the eyes and smacked her lips at me. "You already know where she is at."

"Oh!" I said. My mouth dried up from the thought of her making sure she left me behind so she could get to Papa alone. It pissed me off!

"Papa thinks Lindsay ran off with a pimp," Mama told me.

"A pimp?" I asked, confused. "Why would she do that?"

"Don't ask me!"

"What makes him think that?" I asked, getting my phone out to call her.

Mama grabbed my phone out of my hand and said, "I guess the pimp put a charge on her."

"What?"

"He called Papa and served him her discharge papers," Mama said like it was a normal breakup.

"That girl is not just anybody. I don't want to let her go with some stranger," I cried.

"Trust me. Let her go!" Mama assured me. Then she released my hand. "I've seen so many hos come and go since I have been around."

She was right, but damn. How was it cool to let Lindsay go like that? My feelings were hurt. Lindsay was my friend. I went back and forth in my mind about what would make her leave like that, and the only thing I could think of was Papa fucked her.

I knew it sounded crazy, but I was going crazy! Every date I did since Papa reminded me of Papa. I thought about him when I would daydream; I smelled his cologne when he was not around. I laid down on the double bed, and soon as Mama came into the room, she cuddled up next to me. I can't lie, feeling Mama cuddled up next to me filled up that empty void in my heart, and I could tell she needed hers filled up as well.

"Did you do good last night?" Mama asked me, running her fingers through my hair.

"I did okay," I admitted. "I made over six hundred but gambled a little."

"A little?"

"Okay, a lot!" I laughed.

"Did you have fun?"

"I did have fun."

"I should've been with you then!" she laughed. "I got beat on!"

"That's not funny!"

"I would rather it be me than anyone else."

"Why you say that?"

"I don't like when Papa puts his hands on you girls," she said.

There wasn't anything I could say. All I could do was admire the way she sacrificed herself for us all. She was so sweet.

"Mama?"

"What, love?"

"Remember you said you was going to leave him that one time?" I asked. "Why haven't you?"

She didn't say anything at first, like she had to think and choose her words carefully. Then she said, "I wouldn't know where else to go. I would be somewhere lost, probably getting high if it weren't for Papa. He saved my life!"

"But don't you think you deserve better?" I asked.

"Papa is my best friend. My only friend," she said. "We are a team. I can be myself with him, and we talk about everything. I love him!"

"Everything?" I asked, feeling weird.

"Everything!" she confirmed. "You have to realize that this is not like a boyfriend and girlfriend relationship. Papa is a pimp! There are things you would have to understand about the game before you could understand him. Once you do, you understand why he has to be so cold at times or talk the way he talks to us at times. He is responsible for us. We are players on his team. He coaches us."

"I guess."

"Think about it," she said. "I bet you couldn't tell him how much money you have made altogether since you been with him."

I thought about it, and she was right. "Maybe not."

"Okay, an easier one!" she said, "I bet you don't know how many dates you've done since you've been with him."

"I never looked at it like that," I admitted.

"We're just like basketball players who don't keep track of how many shots they take or how many points they make. All they care about is winning! Not getting hurt and not fouling out of the game. Look at Lindsay!"

"What about her?"

"She wanted to leave the team for another one. Maybe she will get a starting position or even be captain of another team. Maybe she will make more money. Who knows! All I know is that some players get traded from team to team because they don't fit in anywhere. Then you have the players like me, who would never play for another team. Before I do that, I would retire my jersey," she said. "I am loyal to my teammates, to my fans, and to the game."

"I never looked at it that way before," I admitted. "Where did you learn all this?"

"Guess?"

"Papa?"

"Of course! He knows the players before they do their first date. He has seen so many bitches come and go that he will tell me before they make the move. He made sure Lindsay gave me all her money."

"She made money?" I asked curiously.

"Hell yeah! Over a thousand!"

"Damn! So she was a good bitch?"

"No, not really," Mama said. "She was a minor, and all the money in the world wouldn't get Papa out of trouble if she would have got caught with him. I bet he was glad to see her go!"

Mama was right. Maybe Papa was glad to see her leave. Now that I thought about it, so was I. Lindsay was now on the opposite team, and I was happy for her. Besides, what was I going to do about it?

After Mama and I got done talking about the game, Monica busted into the room, letting the door slam. Then she screamed for us to wake up. She was so excited we didn't know what to think.

"Look!" she screamed, throwing a huge sack of exotic weed on the nightstand next to our bed. The she pulled out a different sack of powder.

"Damn, bitch!" Mama yelled, jumping up at the sight of the cocaine. The weed didn't move her, but that powder was like Christmas coming early.

"I robbed him!" Monica yelled nervously. She was shook up, I could tell. Then she pulled out what looked to be a credit card and a bunch of money.

"Damn, how much you take from him?" I asked.

"I actually took the max out of the ATM. He was so drunk that he gave me the card and the PIN number. He is going to kill me if he finds me."

"Girl, why did you do this?" Mama asked after first taking a bump with her nail. The cocaine made her paranoid. "This shit is good as hell. How much do you think it is?"

"I don't know, an ounce maybe."

Marcos came into the room with his phone to his ear. "Okay," he said. "Here!"

"Hello?" Monica said after taking the phone from Marcos. "I hear you!"

She hung up the phone and threw it at Marcos hard enough for it to sound like it hurt. "Snitch!"

"Fuck you, bitch! Them mothafuckas could come kill us all over this shit!" he yelled, at the same time grabbing a huge bud out of the bag. We had run out of piff on the way to Atlantic City.

"I hate you!" she told him on his way out the door.

"Here," Mama told me, handing me a hundred-dollar bill that she had rolled up. "Try it!"

I thought about it and took a little bump. The first time I did coke was with Ricky. He thought he was Tony Montana or some shit. He did so much more coke than he sold, I couldn't understand how he made money. He had to be doing something right.

"This shit is strong as hell," I said.

"He said it was from Columbia," Monica said, jumping in. After she took a huge line, she handed Mama the cards, the money, and the weed. Only thing she kept was the coke.

Mama didn't say shit. She put the money in her Dooney bag. I gave her my money, and then Story came out of nowhere and did the same. I guess I understood, because nobody knew how much money was in her bag, not even her. This was a team, and from the looks of the mound of money she had in her bag, we won the game.

I was so high that I had to go take a cold shower. The cocaine actually helped. It made me want to be alone.

When I came out of the shower, Monica was still up in the corner sitting at the table in front of a few lines. She was extremely high, and from the look of it, she was nervous.

"Where did Mama go?" I asked.

"She probably went to go find some baking soda and a glass dick to smoke out of!" she chuckled. "Crackhead bitch!"

"That was mean!"

"So what? Sue me," she said, shrugging her shoulders and then taking a huge line.

I was drying off with nothing else on except my thong. Monica was outside of her body, and I wasn't about to feed into her attitude.

I laid down and closed my eyes. The smell of the exotic weed was flowing into the room from Marcos and Story's room. I wanted to hit it but decided not to. If I needed to do anything, it was get some rest.

CHAPTER 17

I woke up to the sound of Papa's voice. Him, Mama, and Liz were all sitting at the table. Monica was in the bed next to me as far away as she could get without falling off. She was still dressed and on top of the covers, but she was sound asleep.

Liz and Mama were both up and dressed. They were doing lines off of each other's titties while Papa sat in front of the laptop ignoring them. Story played asleep on the other bed.

"What time is it?" I asked.

"Time for you to get the fuck up and ready!" Papa snapped without looking up from the screen.

Instead of saying what I wanted to, I just smacked my lips and got up, exposing my bare chest, and then went into the bathroom, slamming the door behind me. My head was pounding from the drinks and the coke I did earlier.

I looked at myself in the mirror and couldn't help but scream at the top of my lungs. The makeup, the hickey I couldn't explain, and my puffy sleepless eyes were starting to wear on me.

"Girl, what is wrong with you?" Papa yelled. "You going to have the police up here thinking you're hurt!"

I ignored him. When I came out of the bathroom, everyone was up and looking at me. This was not the time to fuck with me.

"You need to calm down," Liz said to me.

"Bitch, you need to mind your fucking business!" I yelled. Everyone looked at me. There wasn't a sound in the room besides my heart pounding in my chest.

Papa said, "Sit down!"

I sat. Then I said, "Tell your little princess to stay the fuck out of my way!" Then I rolled my eyes.

He didn't say anything to me. Instead he addressed Liz and said, "Leave her alone!"

The rest of them all smacked their lips in unison. They knew I deserved to be slapped for the way I was acting. Hell, I knew I needed to be smacked or fucked or something! I got my bag and went to finish getting dressed.

I was flat-ironing my hair, listening to Miguel on my iPhone, when someone knocked on the door. I ignored it. I was pissed off for a reason only I knew. I didn't want to talk to anyone.

"Bitch, open up this door!" Papa said in a low but serious tone.

I unlocked the door and then continued to do my hair. He came in with a blunt in his hand.

"Thank you," I said after handing him the blunt back.

"What's wrong with you?" he asked me, already knowing the answer.

"Nothing," I lied.

"We about to go out to eat and shopping before y'all go to work tonight," he said.

"That's sweet of you."

"Bitch, I know you ain't catching no feelings!"

"Never that," I mumbled under my breath. "I am cool. I am a woman, and at times we go through things. I'm sure I will get over it!"

"You better hurry up and get over it," he said. Then someone knocked on the door.

"Go," I said, rolling my eyes.

He instantly grabbed the back of my neck, causing me to accidentally but on purpose touch his hand with the flat iron. He didn't flinch, but I could tell it hurt because he squeezed harder on my neck.

A tear came to my eye, but it didn't fall. He looked coldly into my eyes in the mirror from behind me and then let go with a slight push.

"Hurry up!" he said and then left.

Soon as he left, the tear I'd barely held on to fell. It was the only one I had left. Other than that, my heart was cold as ice and dry as the desert. I heard them all making noises as they left the room. I didn't care if they left me behind or not, but I still hurried up so that I could, if possible, join the little shopping spree. I deserved at least that much.

To my surprise, when I finally came out of the bathroom dressed in a pair of black leggings, a black long-sleeve shirt, and a pair of black flip flops, I saw that I wasn't alone. Monica was in the adjacent room also getting dressed. She didn't look like she was getting dressed to go shopping either; she looked like she was about to go to work.

"Girl, why aren't you with them?" I asked.

"I don't have time to splurge and party around. A bitch got work to do," she said, causing me to envy her work ethic.

"But you made all that money last night."

"What does that mean?" she asked while she laced up her new boots. She was putting on a black short dress, some fishnet panty hose, and the boots that came up to her thighs. She looked damn good.

"You look nice!" I said. "Where did you get that new outfit?"

"Daddy buys and picks out all of my clothes for me. I never even have to ask, he just knows what I need and gets it for me," she said with a smile. "The boots came from Aldos and the dress from Be Be, and he even got me another bottle of Dolce and Gabanna Light Blue. He always likes when I wear Dolce Light Blue."

"Um . . ." was all I could say. Deep down inside, I wanted to say more. Instead of going there, I said, "Be careful out there, girl!"

"Please! I know what I'm doing. You do me a favor and don't let this game get to you. There have been many times when I wanted to snap, even kill myself, but you have to be strong because only the strong survive."

The last comment Monica made to me as I was leaving really stuck with me. It was what I needed to hear. I was acting weak and spoiled, and for what? Nobody cared.

We parked down the strip at the Ceasars casino parking lot. Of all the places we had to come back to, it was the place where I spent all night working in. Papa gave me, Mama, and Story $250 each before we got out of the car.

"Go to the mall on the boardwalk and then meet me in the poker room when y'all get done," he said.

We all looked at one another and then, without hesitation, got out of the van. Marcos followed us, but at a distance. He had a lot of money saved up; he had been getting $125 a day for driving, so he had a couple thousand of his own. All he did was shop. Even when we weren't around, he would find places to buy little things for his kids along the way.

The Ceasars mall was nice. It sat right on the boardwalk. It was a huge green glass building—we could see it from our hotel-room balcony, but I'd never known what it was.

We had a blast, too. This was the first time we'd all hung out this way, just having fun. Mama led the way pretty much the whole time. Liz had her own money, so she was a little more free to buy whatever she wanted, but she didn't spend nearly as much as us. She seemed pissed when Papa didn't give her money to shop with. I was shocked about it too. I guess being his "little princess" wasn't all that special. The whole time we were at home waiting on her, and she was flying back home the next day. Just hearing her constantly talking about home was making my blood boil. I wanted to slap her mouth shut. She was just mad.

After we all got cute black dresses and boots, we pitched in and got Papa a New Jersey Nets hat with a jersey to match. Liz was so desperate to outdo us all that she bought him a pair of Michael Jordans to match. Mama was happy she got him some shoes, but it pissed me off. I hated being outdone by her. Story couldn't care less. She was so detached from her feelings, I doubt if she even noticed us all compete the way we did for his attention.

Once we finally met back up with Papa by the poker room, he was done playing. From the smile on his face and the way he hugged Mama, we could tell he must have won at least some of the money back that he lost at the Borgata.

"Where do you all want to eat?" he asked when we got back in the van. "We could walk up to the strip or Atlantic and choose between Ruby Tuesday, Ruth's Chris, or The Melting Pot."

"I want to go to Ruby Tuesday, Daddy," Liz said. "I love when we make our own salads."

"Bitch, don't nobody want no salad," Story said, sweetly but in a serious voice. Liz pouted.

"Papa, you pick," Mama said. She knew how to always say the right thing.

"Cuz," Marcos interrupted. He had been smoking a blunt by himself when we got in the van. "I can drop you all off, and then I am going to Popeye's."

"That's cool," Papa said, taking the blunt and passing it to Mama. "Drop us off at Indiana and Atlantic City."

By the time the blunt made its way around, we were getting dropped off. The crowd here was totally different from the crowd on the boardwalk. Black people were everywhere we turned. We left all the bags, except the stuff we bought Papa, in the van.

I could tell by the looks on all the faces along the strip that they were used to seeing pimps and hos. Guys nodded their hats off to Papa Bear, while girls turned their noses up at us. It was getting late and a little chilly outside.

"Kassie!" I heard a familiar voice yell from across the street.

Papa looked over to the Greyhound station the same time I did. It was Lindsay, standing out front, trying to get my attention. I didn't know what to do at first, so instead of doing anything, I looked away and into Papa's eyes.

"Kassie!" she yelled again, this time waving her arms in the air. There wasn't anything I could do. I didn't even look back.

We walked into The Melting Pot just in time. It took everything inside of me not to burst into tears and run over to Lindsay. Papa noticed—hell, so did everyone else. I still wonder what he would've done if I did go see what she wanted, or if I even would've spoke. I left my friend hanging. I chose!

The hostess put us in a secluded private room in the back of the restaurant. It was nice as hell, but it was a way to hide us from the upper-class crowd that was in attendance.

Soon as we got into the room, Liz practically pushed me down to try to get the seat to the right of Papa. I was closest to him, so I was the closest to the seat.

I looked Liz square in the eyes. She was ready to throw down for her position. I was too!

"Daddy, I bought this for you!" she yelled in my face, holding his shoes up in my face.

"Kassie, baby," Mama said. "Come sit next to me so I can show you how this whole fondue thing works."

As bad as I wanted to spit in Liz's face, I just made my way all the way around the table to sit next to Mama. Story even moved out of her seat so I could sit down. She was smiling at me the whole time. Papa smiled too, but at Story. They had this real father-daughter type of relationship that was hard to explain. There was more to them two. I just couldn't figure it out. I respected it, though. She was loyal to him and minded her own business.

Papa ordered for us all. He ordered "The Big Night Out," which was a four-course fondue experience. It came with a house salad, Wisconsin trio cheese, and turtle chocolate. For all of our meals, he ordered us the Land and Sea, which came with steak, chicken, and shrimp.

The food was delicious. We all took turns sharing and dipping breadsticks, Granny Smith apples, and strawberries. The experience was one to remember. Papa still treated me like I was sitting next to him, because it was my first time. He cooked all my meats for me, and he poured all of our Moscato for us. We had a total of five bottles of Moscato sparkling wine.

After we finished eating, we walked down to the Club 40/40 on the corner. It was just opening, so none of us had to show identification. We had a blast, too! We drank Top Shelf Margaritas, and everyone danced except me and Papa.

"I guess Lindsay going home?" Papa asked me.

"I guess."

"You did good," he said.

Feeling the drinks, I asked, "I did good not speaking to my friend?"

"I know it was hard, but it showed me a lot," he said, lifting his glass up to give me a toast.

After our little talk, Mama came up and dragged me onto the dance floor. She had a few country-singing guys who were going to perform later on at the club who were interested in us all. I just went with the flow. I was full, and the only thing I wanted was to smoke a blunt. Lucky for me, because they wanted some coke, and we had just what they were looking for.

We met Marcos back at the same spot he had dropped us off at. The guys were staying at the Sheridan off the strip, so we knew where they would be, but from the look on Marcos's face, we had another problem.

"Cuz!" he told Papa.

"What?"

"It's Monica!"

"What about her?"

"Man, Cuz, she fucked up," he said.

We all listened. None of us wanted to hear any of that.

When we got to the room, first thing we saw was her dress on the ground. She was under the covers crying, naked. I don't know what pissed Papa off more, but he snatched the covers off of the bed and exposed her beat-up body. She had bruises all over her body like she had been beaten with a pole or bat, and her right eye was swollen shut.

"Bitch, what the fuck are you doing?" Papa yelled.

"I am beat-up, Daddy!"

"No, you are laying up feeling sorry for yourself!"

We all looked at each other and then at her. She was bleeding from her asshole, and her jaw was looking like a plum.

"What do you want me to do? They found me and beat and raped me. They took turns fucking me in the ass, Daddy!" she yelled.

"Did you get any more money?"

"Are you serious?"

"Bitch, do I look like I am playing?" he snapped. "Get up and soak in the tub for a minute and get dressed. You have a date, bitch!"

"I can't go, Daddy!" she pleaded. "Please don't make me go!"

"Don't make me tell you again."

She could barely get up from out of the bed. Mama jumped to her and helped her into the bathroom. Monica cried so hard my throat caught a lump in it. There wasn't anything I could do or say to help, as bad as I wanted to. I just stood there staring at the monster in front of me.

I followed him out onto the balcony. At first I didn't know what to say, so I just came out with it.

"I wanted to leave you," I said.

"What stopped you?" he asked while holding the smoke in his lungs from the blunt.

"I don't know," I admitted.

"Well, next time, do me a favor and do it," he said. Then he smacked me on the ass. "Now get dressed and make a play."

For some reason, I felt good about telling him I almost left him. He got the point I was making, and I got his. I think it was our mutual understanding that made me more eager than ever to go to work. He wasn't that bad of a person, it was just business, and the only thing that mattered was making money. Great ballplayers play injured all the time. They play because their teammates need them. We needed her.

Chapter 18

The next morning, we left to take Liz to the Philadelphia airport. We all had partied extremely hard the night before; the country singers sent us a party bus to pick us up, full of drinks. Soon as they finished their performance, they joined us.

Nobody paid Monica's beat-up face any attention. They actually liked her the most, I guess because she was the one carrying all the cocaine. She carried herself very well considering the circumstances, too.

Mama did Monica's makeup very well. She blended blush into her cheeks, put dark eye shadow on her eyes, and even let her wear her large-lens Gucci frames. Monica looked more like a diva than she ever had before, and she played the part well.

As expected, the lead singer picked Mama. The rest of them really didn't care about anything but the coke, and they ended up purchasing all of it.

Sam and I talked about him coming to meet me in Philly for a couple hours in the King of Prussia area at this hotel called Dolce. Papa didn't mind at all, so he dropped me off at the room before they took Liz to the airport. The hotel was beautiful. It was a boutique-style hotel, very lavish and upscale. Sam drove from Delaware and beat me there, so he was already in the room when I arrived.

"Hi there!" he greeted me as I entered the room. He was wearing a business suit like he left work just to come join me. "I couldn't stop thinking about you!"

"That's sweet!" I said, sitting down in front of the window. The last day or so had changed me so much that I had this no-nonsense type of aura about myself.

"You okay?" he asked me, immediately dropping to his knees and taking one of my battered feet into his hands. He rubbed my feet from the ankle down, both of them.

"I'm fine!"

Sam picked me up off the plush chair and carried me over to the king-size bed. I let him do what he wanted to me. My body was his for the taking. I never asked about money or time; all I did was lay there.

He stripped me down to nothing and then stopped. I was trembling from trying not to burst into tears. I was not there mentally, but physically and emotionally I was.

Sam noticed this and instead of pushing any further, he took his shorts off and lay next to me and held me. I cried into his chest again.

"No," I whispered.

"No what, sweetheart?" he asked.

"Don't stop."

He looked at me for a long moment. Then he laid me back down and took his time kissing me all over my body. His touch, his lips, the smell of his cologne were unique. I was with Sam, and I wanted to use him to get Papa out of my mind.

Sam made love to me. It was so passionate and intense that I must of climaxed several times. My body needed this. I was so sexually frustrated.

Soon as we finished, Sam got dressed and left. Before he left, he gave me a long kiss on my forehead. For some reason, it felt like this would be the last time I ever saw him. Love-making and climaxing were forbidden in this game. So not seeing Sam again wouldn't be the worst thing that could happen to me.

After getting picked up I just handed over the sealed envelope to Papa and got into the back of the van and laid down. Monica was laid out on the floor, Marcos was driving with Papa in the passenger seat, and Mama and Story were both in the back reclining chairs, asleep as well.

We rode for a while in silence. I hit the blunt a couple of times, but other than that, I kept my head down in the back.

Papa texted my phone and said, "You hungry?"

"Yes," I texted back.

"What's wrong with you?"

"I am okay," I texted.

"You better be!"

"I don't feel like playing right now," I texted.

"Fuck you too, then!"

"You don't get it."

"You want to go shopping?" he texted.

"I am tired of shopping! I am tired of all this shit!" I texted.

"So you ready to go home?"

"Did I say that?" I asked.

"Then what do you want?"

"Honestly?"

"This is the time to speak up!" he texted.

"I want to go see my little sister. I want to be around some real love, not none of this fake shit around here!"

"Anything else?"

"Yes," I said. "I want to spend some time with you, just you for a change."

"That's what we are doing now," he said.

"Fuck you!"

"Where is your little sister?"

"Florida," I said. "Tampa Bay."

Soon after Papa and I finished our alone-time texting, we arrived at a strip in the heart of Philly. I looked at the street sign and saw it was South Street and Broad. Everyone woke up to the sound of loud music and the smell of food that floated into the van as we rode down the tightly packed street. People carelessly walked directly in front of the van as if they had bumpers.

"There!" Papa pointed to a place on the corner called Jim's Original Steaks. There was a line clear out the door. "That's what I want!"

"I'll go," Story said, jumping up. Papa handed her some money. "What do you want?"

"Get me a Philly with some onions and Cheez Whiz," he said, licking his lips.

"What's Cheez Whiz?" Story asked.

"It's like nacho cheese. They will know what you mean," he said. "And get pizza sauce on the side."

"I'm coming!" Mama yelled, getting out with Story.

Monica finally got up, looking a mess. She glanced up and down the street. I just watched her. Her eye was worse—now purple as well as black.

"Oh, oh," she said. "Daddy, can I go get my fortune told?"

"Me too!" I yelled. I grew up watching Cleo on television and always wanted to know the future.

Ignoring us both, Papa pulled out a hundred-dollar bill and handed it back. Then he said, "Hurry up, and don't bring that witchcraft back into this car with y'all!"

Monica and I took off down the street. Everyone noticed her eye because she wasn't wearing glasses or makeup anymore. It was so embarrassing.

We made it halfway down the block to the first of many fortune readers. We picked this particular one because it said she did two for one: tarot cards and palm reading. Monica went first, so I stayed outside smoking a cigarette. When she came storming out minutes later crying, I was scared to go in, but she assured me it was okay.

I walked inside and up the stairs to what seemed to be a trap. There was incense burning as well as candles. I felt a chill run up my spine.

"Have a seat," the older lady said to me as I looked around. She wore a scarf around her head with another one covering her mouth so I couldn't see her lips. I couldn't see her at all from the black paint on the walls, making the flickering candlelight cast shadows.

"Is this good?" I asked, sitting down across from her in a wicker chair. There was a cushion between us on the floor. The instant I sat down, what seemed to be a black cat rubbed against my leg. I jumped.

"Calm down!" she yelled, causing me to jump again. "It is important to be absolutely quiet! I do all the talking here. Close your eyes and give me your hand."

I did as she said. Her hands seemed large for a lady and her voice was deeper than normal for a lady, but I went on with it, shivering in her hand.

She rubbed the lines inside my hand, tickling me, which gave my body the excuse it needed to tremble freely.

"I see! I see!" she said. "These hands of yours belong to a man. These hands of yours perform the works of evildoing!"

"I . . ."

"Shhh!" she stopped me, squeezing even harder to keep me in my seat. "These hands of yours have touched many skins! These hands of yours are hurt!"

The more she read my hands, the more full of shit I thought she was. There were some obvious things she must be able to tell.

"These hands of yours hold a dark secret! These hands of yours have no past or future!"

With that said, I snatched my hand away. I was going to leave when she stopped me.

"This is hard because the truth hurts," she said, laughing out loud. "There is more! Dare to let me read your tarot?"

I stopped in my tracks. The only light I saw was from the stairway. I turned back toward the flickering shadow and said, "You're full of shit!"

"Then let me finish, please. There is more!" she said. I heard the shuffling of cards.

I sat back down, and she shoved the deck into my hands. "You mix these up and hand them back to me."

I did. I mixed them up as much as I could. I was no longer trembling. I was sure this was a scam.

"Okay!" she said. "Now take one and keep it, but don't look at it. I will pull the same card as you!"

I took out a card, and she did too. "Now what?" I asked.

"Look at this," she said, holding her card up to the flickering light. It was a picture of a stork, a bird carrying a baby in its mouth.

I turned over my card and it was the same. "Bullshit!"

"You are with child, my dear!" she said. "The child is a secret. You must never tell a soul!"

"Why not? I have a son! What type of shit is this?"

"The session is now done! Please leave!"

I picked up the pillow and tossed it at the wall. Then I stormed out of the place, but stopped at the top of the stairs and asked, "Why not tell?"

"Please leave!" she said, and then she started laughing again.

I fell down the stairs trying to run out, barely catching my balance. The sunlight seemed to blind me. The once friendly crowd seemed to all be staring at me. The van seemed far away.

Stumbling up to the open door on the side of the van, I saw everyone smiling and enjoying their food. The sight of them mixed with the smell of onions was too much to bear. I threw up all over the ground. Everyone stopped eating and looked at me with disgust.

"Nasty bitch!" Papa said.

"You okay?" Mama said, jumping out to help me. She grabbed some of her napkins out of her bag of food and handed them to me.

"I am fine!" I lied. "The onions made me gag."

111

"Gross!" Story said, balling her food up and throwing it onto the ground out of the open door rudely.

Next thing I knew, we were back on the road, crossing a huge bridge out of Philly. All of them finished eating their food like I wasn't even present. The music was still off.

"What did that witch say to you?" Monica asked, talking with a mouthful of food.

"Nothing really," I lied. "I think she or it or whatever it was, was full of shit!"

"Me too!" Monica said, smacking her lips. "Bitch had the nerve to tell me that I was jealous of one of my coworkers and that I lived my life trying to be someone I could never amount to!"

"That's why you left so fast?" I asked.

"No, the evil bitch told me to get out and gave me my money back."

"Damn! I never even paid her myself," I said, feeling bad.

"Bitch, I told you not to bring all that voodoo in here!" Papa yelled.

"Sorry!" Monica said sarcastically. Then she looked at me with a smile.

"Papa, where we going?" Mama asked, still eating and feeding him at the same time. She was sitting on the floor next to him in the front seat while Marcos drove.

"Florida," Papa said, putting the GPS up in the window, searching for the address he put in. "Tampa Bay."

"Florida?" Monica asked, shocked. "How far is that?"

"Where you got to be?" he asked her.

"Cuz, you serious?" Marcos asked, looking away from the road into Papa's eyes.

"Yeah! Why? You need me to drive?"

"Not yet, but shit, eventually!"

The whole car went silent. I was probably the only person who knew why we were heading that far out of the way. Anyway, we all needed a vacation or a break. I knew I did.

"Thank you," I texted Papa.

"Thank me later!" he texted back.

"I will!"

Chapter 19

The drive to Tampa was at least twice as long as the drive to New York from Indiana. We didn't do much stopping along the way, but one stop we made was to cross on the Cape May Ferry. Crossing the Delaware River was my very first time being in a boat. It was beautiful, too! The sun was setting, creating an orange glaze across the horizon. The seagulls followed in the wake of the murky water, and the passengers all smiled and enjoyed life the way I had always dreamed I would one day.

Other than the beautiful sights and bridges we passed and crossed along the way, the trip was long and boring. The only thing that kept me awake the majority of the time was the thought of seeing my little sister, Jackie, again—after Lord knows how many years it had been.

We checked into the Days Inn near the Tampa Bay Buccaneers stadium. We got two rooms next to each other, one to work in and the other for us to stay in. This was the first time Papa stayed in the room with us all, which was weird. It was like having a parent or guardian around; all of us were on our best behavior.

It was pretty late when we pulled into Tampa. The strip that our rooms were on was lit up. There were three strip clubs within walking distance of our room, a Walmart across the road, and restaurants lined up and down the strip.

"Papa!" Mama yelled, excited. "Can I try to get a dancing job at Mons Venus?"

"Then what?" he asked.

"I don't know! I just heard it was a nice club to work in," she said, still excited. "Remember when I told you that I came here years ago with my friend and she had a millionaire trick that she met that bought her a Jag?"

"I remember you telling me about the guy that had you working for him, too!" he snapped. He was on the laptop posting ads for us on the Internet. "Not tonight!"

"Papa *jealous*," she sarcastically joked with him, at the same time reaching over from where she sat on the edge of the bed and touching his hand.

Papa jerked away from her and startled everybody, including Marcos, who was at the same table rolling up the last of the exotic weed up. "Get dressed!" Papa demanded, not to one but to all of us. "We going traditional tonight. Then, if you do good, I don't mind you dancing the rest of the time we are here."

"Okay, Papa," Mama said. She always got her way one way or another. I think it's just that Papa believed in her so much that he knew she would make money no matter what she did. I was hesitant to ask Papa about going to see my sister. She had already texted me the address where she lived. I really didn't want to get all hookered up and then go see her, but if that was the only way, I would. My sister knew me.

I texted him, "Papa, can I have Marcos take me to visit my little sister really fast?"

He looked at his phone and read the text. Without replying or anything, he put the phone back into his pocket and continued working online. I smacked my lips and then got up and went to the room next door to get dressed, but before I left I slammed the door to the room as hard as I could.

I took my time getting dressed. The fact that we were working didn't bother me. Hell, I knew what time it was. This is what we did. But I also thought there should be a time when a bitch gets a break.

Coming to Florida was supposed to be about me coming to see my sister, or so I had thought.

I put on a dress; it was really skimpy. It was black, made of silk-type fabric that formed to my petite frame just right. The back was out, and I put curls in my hair so that it looked like I had pretty long locks.

Papa was in the room alone waiting for me when I came out of the bathroom. My shoes were not on, but other than that, I was fully dressed.

"You look nice," he said. He was also dressed up in a tight-fitting button-up shirt, designer slacks, and some black alligator shoes he bought in Philly. They were nice. His whole outfit was navy blue and dark blue.

"You look damn good yourself!" I said, and he did.

I stepped up to him and took his white Kangol hat off of his head and sat it on top of mine. He picked me up by my legs and sat me on his lap in one of the chairs at the table, and then he said, "You need to stop acting up!"

"Well, stop ignoring me all the time."

"I don't be ignoring you," he said. Then he kissed me deep and long, for the first time easing his tongue into my mouth.

He kissed me so good that my juices started to flow. His tongue tasted like sour candy. "You already been drinking?"

"I had one margarita across the parking lot at the Mexican bar," he said. "Why?"

"Nothing! You taste like it," I said, getting up off of his lap. My shoes were in the box they came in on the bed. I slipped into them and kept talking. "So, am I going to get to see my sister or what?"

"Um-um!" he moaned, looking at me. His eyes weakened my knees. He turned me on so much I couldn't help it.

"You like what you see?" I mumbled.

He grabbed my hand and rubbed it against his slacks. He was bulging through his pants. Then he mumbled back, "Do you have a taste for my pimp juice?"

Without another word, I unzipped his dark pants, letting me see his huge cock jump through the hole in his brand-new white boxers. I took his hat off and sat it on top of his head. Then I squatted down on my heels at the edge of the bed and took him into my mouth. Soon as I did, there was a light knock at the door. I started to stop, but Papa nearly choked me with his dick forcing me back down on him.

After a few more strokes, Papa stood up and bent me over the bed, lifting my tight skirt up over my ass, barely ripping my panties as he pulled them to the side. Then he bent down and used his tongue to lick my pussy lips around the entrance. Papa was such an animal when he wanted inside. When he stood up, he seemed to stand straight up inside of me. The first thrust did hurt a little from him being rough, but after the first stroke inside me, I began to cum.

The light knocks on the door turned into pounds. Whoever was at the door knew what was going on, so when he kept pounding my pussy, forcefully slapping me on my ass, I screamed as loud as I could. The door pound was hard, so I yelled louder, and Papa smacked my ass harder.

The heels made it perfect for Papa to reach my G-spot. I screamed one last time, in chorus with Papa's loud grunt and the obvious kick to the door. Then all went silent. He stayed where he was until the very last drop of his nut was inside of me.

It felt great, his warm juices flowing inside of me. The scene! The sex! I was in heaven!

I ran to the sink and watched Papa through the mirror as I used a towel to wash my pussy off. He wasn't paying me any attention; it was like he knew what to expect, because he didn't make any attempt to fix his own pants up or nothing. He was texting somebody from his phone. I lathered up a towel and went over to him and washed him up. He was still texting but also reacting to my touch. He was starting to grow hard again; I finished by one last time taking him into my mouth, making a popping sound as I stroked him one last time. He came too late and finished fixing himself up.

"Want a drink?" he asked me, while at the same time cracking open the door to the room.

Before I could answer, Mama walked in. She wasn't showing me any signs. She said, "You look good, sexy mama!"

"Thank you," I said. "Look at you!"

She was dressed up in a sexy form-fitting one-piece outfit. Her belly was out, showing her belly ring, and the back of her outfit had a hood attached. Hers was real silk, and it matched her red-bottom heels great!

"Monica is in the other room doing a date," she told Papa.

"Is that who was pounding on the door?" he asked.

"She said she needed the room key for a date. Marcos and Story are in the van."

"That's good!" he said. "You want a drink, Mama?"

"I could eat!"

"Me too," I said.

Without another word to me, Mama and Papa walked over to the Mexican restaurant/bar. I ordered a couple of tacos and a Long Island. Mama and Papa shared a sizzling fajita meal. They had a special bond, and I didn't like being between them. I sat next to Papa on one side while Mamma sat on the other side. Papa didn't change one bit after fucking the shit out of me. I guess now I saw why it was so important for a bitch to detach her heart from her pussy.

Sitting in the restaurant watching Mama feed Papa bites of their meal to each other made me sick—literally! I ate a few bites and slammed my drink. Then I went to the restroom to clean myself up. I was leaking from all the cum he had just filled me up with.

Soon as I stepped into the restroom, vile-tasting saliva came into my mouth. Someone else was in the stall next to me, so I tried to hold it in as long as I could, which didn't last too long. I threw up everywhere. I got most of it inside the toilet, but the rest went all over my suede shoes and the floor.

"You okay?" this older white lady asked me. "Seems like you need to stop drinking, honey. You're pregnant!"

I looked at her. She was at least sixty years old, wore an apron around her neck untied, and was a little on the heavy side. Her makeup was heavy, but her voice was still soft and caring. Coming out of the stall and grabbing a handful of paper towels, I said, "I can't be. I can't be! It's no way!"

"Well, if you been having sex, it's very possible. Now, if you are a virgin, then maybe not, but I have eleven granddaughters. I know pregnant when I see it."

"But it's only been a couple weeks or so," I argued.

"Honey, as small as you are, it don't take long before your body gets the signals," she said. And she was right. When I was pregnant with Carlton, I was the same way.

"I don't want it," I blurted out without thinking.

"Sweetheart! Babies are blessings from God. Not wanting them is like not wanting your blessings," she said. "Now, don't worry about this mess. Go ahead! I'll take care of it. Just take care of yourself and that baby of yours."

I took her advice and made my way back to the bar to find our seats empty. Mama and Papa were gone. Once I was alone, guys approached me. I gave my number to a couple and then left.

The van was out front waiting for me. Everybody was inside waiting. Cologne and perfume filled the air as the side door opened. Papa and Monica were in the back in my favorite spot. Mama sat up front to finish her makeup, and Story sat next to me. Sade was playing.

"I met a nice trick at the bar," I told Mama, excited.

"Good baby!"

"He wasn't ready to go now?" Papa asked me rudely.

"I am sure he was, but I told him I would call him later on."

"Bitch, what do you mean you going to call him later?" he snapped like a madman. Then he jumped up over my seat, opened the door for me, and handed me the room key. "Tricks aren't going to wait for your funky ass. By the time we get back, it should be checked out. Go take your lazy ass back up in there and don't come out again ever talking about what you did unless you got some money for me, bitch!"

I was shook up. Papa had some nerve. I did what he said, which worked. The trick didn't have nothing but forty dollars, which I took, but Papa was right. The trick still wanted me to call later on, but Papa was right.

Our first stop was at this club in Ybor City called Prana. It was on 7th Avenue and was really nice. It was my first time being VIP in a club. Papa ordered bottles and Jager bombs. The crowd was nice and young.

All of us girls went to work the crowd while Marcos and Papa sat back. He had four girls with him already. He was chilling with the girls and buying anybody and everybody drinks, but for the most part, his focus was on us.

Monica actually did a date in the VIP, which Papa set up as well. He worked the crowd in the VIP. All the guys knew what he was and approached him. Then he was distributing us to the guys like they'd ordered pizza.

I did a date in the van. Story left in a cab to the room with a date. It was wild. We were all so drunk, including Papa and Marcos, that when we finally left the club heading to another one, no one wanted to drive. Mama ended up driving; she was such a drinker that even after drinking almost a whole bottle of Cîroc, she still seemed sober. We ended up at a club called Hollywood Nights that one of the local guys told Papa about. It was on Howard Avenue, wherever that was. I remember the name of the street because we had to walk almost a mile from where we parked the van. The parking lot was packed.

Papa made us go in first. There was a car full of girls following us from the club, and Marcos rode with them. Papa paid a guy a hundred dollars for his parking space by the door, so while he got that together we went inside.

Now, let me tell you a little about what I saw once I got inside the door. The line out front was so long you couldn't tell that most of the girls in the line had on dance outfits. When we walked into the entrance, there was money flying everywhere! Bitches were everywhere shaking their asses. There were piles of money all over the floor. It was wild.

The bartenders were naked, and they had piles of money on the floor behind the bar as well, and everybody was black. Mama and Monica were the only white bitches in sight. There were more in the back, but for the most part we stood out.

Guys were slapping our asses with money. Guy after guy attacked us. Story loved it! She had on some leather shorts up in her ass, her chest was under a lace bra that could pass for a shirt, and black things came up her back. Before long, she had on nothing but her thong and a pile of money in front of her so big that I almost passed out. This was the first time Story took the lead. All we had to do was follow along. She had about twenty guys throwing money at her to take it all off and before long, she did. She was butt naked, shaking her ass so hard that not only the guys but the bitches too were surrounding us, trying to get in on the action.

The rest of us followed suit, and before Papa and Marcos finally found us we were all naked. I think that was the first time I had ever seen a genuine smile on Papa's face. He shook his head up and down to me. I smiled back. We took over the club.

Mama and some girl from the crowd were dancing on each other. The bitch was a red bone and bad, too. I joined in with them and before long, Mama and I took back over kissing, touching, and fingering each other. We went so far that security came over to us and gave us two buckets for all the money we had on the ground.

The girls who came with Marcos joined in as well, not totally naked like we were, but they had their shirts off and were all over Marcos and Papa. We had a blast! The crowd was respectful, too. They loved Papa Bear. They all took pictures with him and us like we were famous.

After we danced for that first hour or so, we got dressed and chilled in VIP. The security guards let Papa get all the money together, and he gave them a hundred dollars apiece to watch out for him. The club owner sent us a free bottle of Cîroc as well.

This was the life. I was sweating up a storm. So was everybody else. A couple of girls from the crowd tried to choose Papa. This was the first time I had ever seen a bitch choose a pimp—a complete stranger. He didn't seem too excited about it, but he still let them drink and chill with us. The red bone who was all over Mama was the most serious. She made his drinks, held his cup for him, and made only a splash every time using a new cup. He liked her, and so did I.

The thing I really liked the most was how she didn't ask for any of the money we made, and on top of that, she gave him all the money she had made before we got there as well. She was a real ho, but so was we. The bitch was cold. I was tearing!

CHAPTER 20

I woke up next to Red and Monica. Mama, Papa, and Story were on the other bed, knocked out as well. Once we made it back to the hotel room around six in the morning, I took Red with me to the guy's room from the bar, which all worked out because he gave us both a hundred dollars apiece. Red claimed that it was her first real date ever, which I found extremely hard to believe. But anyway, she turned the money over to Papa Bear without thinking twice.

Marcos and the driver of the pack of girls who had been following us around all night were banging the bed against the wall in the work room next door. It just made me embarrassed by the thought of how much noise I had to have been making when Papa fucked me so good the day before.

My plan was to get up early and try to get Marcos to take me to see my sister before all the chaos started, but from the sound of it, he was busy. I got up anyway. As I looked around the room at Papa laying between Mama and Story, and then at Monica laying naked out in the open, and last but not least at Red as she snored ever so lightly, my stomach did a flip upside down. Red was very pretty. Her hair was long with bright red highlights in it. She wasn't petite, but she wasn't big either. She had big boobs, but her ass wasn't no bigger than mine, and that not much. She had sex appeal.

"What you doing up?" Mama asked me. She was still laying on Papa's belly, his wifebeater lifted up. "Come here!"

I went over to her, and she reached out to me so that I could lay next to her. Papa rolled away from her, spooning Story as Mama did the same to me. Only thing I could think about was how bad I wished I was in Story's position.

The Florida sunshine gleamed into our room so brightly that it was hard to close my eyes facing the window. I looked around at everything as if it were the face of reality. The sound of water splashing from the pool outside our room, the sound of kids running down the walkway, playing, laughing, crying—it was all too much to bear. The tears I'd been holding back for days forced their way down my cheeks.

I got up and went to use the restroom as quietly as I could. Even when I puked, I tried to do it silently, but I couldn't. I should've eaten more or something. Those shots and drinks and dancing made me extra sick. When I puked, nothing came out. I had to make a grunting noise to help me get it out.

The door swung open, and of all the people or times to interrupt, it was Papa. He frowned at me and asked, "Bitch, are you pregnant?"

I said, "No," but him and I both knew the truth. I tried to clean it up by saying, "I am hungover."

"Bitch, you barely drunk shit! I been watching your funky ass. This the third time you done got sick in a row. You better the fuck not be pregnant!"

Fed up, I asked, "Or what?" I was still bent over the toilet and still wearing my skirt from last night.

The first kick almost took my life. I just knew it. And if I wasn't dead, I knew my baby was going to be soon. He used all his might and again kicked me one last time in my stomach. Then he picked my limp body up by my hair and flung me out of the bathroom into the room.

The agony, the pain was so unbearable that I couldn't yell, and I couldn't breathe. Before I could grasp my first breath, he was kicking me again, this time in my pussy, between my legs. I was on my knees trying to crawl away, throwing up everywhere, and I even think there was blood. I could no longer hear shit. He was now punching the side of my head into the ground. I saw all of the girls trying to save me, except for Red. She held my gaze as I started to black out. She was cuffing a pillow on the bed.

"Bitch, I will kill you and that trick's baby!" he yelled, now held down by Mama and Marcos.

"How am I pregnant with a trick's baby? If your nasty dick ass wasn't fucking all up in my pussy, this wouldn't have happened," I tried to say but could barely talk. I was barely alive. I lay face down to avoid the exchange of stares. Monica, Story, and Red were all hugged up together as if they had heard it all. All were hugging the pillow or each other.

The room phone started ringing. Nobody moved. The cat was out of the bag. Papa now done heard it all. He busted free and kicked me again one last time, which was the last thing I saw. I remember him lifting me up off the ground, or was that part of a dream?

When I finally woke up, I was in his arms. We were in the back of the van laying on the let-out bed. I tried to jump up to see around, but the pain was too unbearable to move. He pulled me back down. "Shh!"

I gargled, "Where are we going?" I could barely talk. My mouth was swollen up so bad that I couldn't open my lips all the way.

"Miami," he whispered while rubbing the hair from my face.

I busted into tears. "What about my sister?"

"Shh!" he said again, but this time with more authority.

I looked up again and saw that Red was in the front seat with Marcos. Story was crying in one of the recliners. Monica was playing asleep with her Mickey Mouse blanket over her head. Mama was missing.

"Where is Mama?" I asked out loud, finally lifting up.

"That devil left her," Story screamed.

"What?" I said, looking into his cold eyes.

He reached over to the ground and lifted up Mama's red-bottom heel from the night before. Then he said, "I hope you can fit these, because you have some large shoes to fill." Then he had the nerve to smile.

I couldn't believe my eyes. Was this what this shit was all about? I didn't give a fuck about being his bottom bitch. I much would've rather been his baby mama. Fuck this shit.

The first punch caught him square in his face. The next few blows went wild, but it didn't matter. It was too late to get beat on. I was ready to die. I swung so many times until I couldn't swing anymore, and just like the punk he was to kick and hit me, he balled up and let me swing. He took every one of them. It was the best feeling in the world, too. The very first time I balled up my fist and punched anyone in my life.

"I hate you!" I screamed. "Why?"

"I deserved that," he said.

We were pulling up to a hotel called the Seagull Inn. The street sign said 21st and Collins Avenue. Nobody was as excited to be in Miami as Red. She started talking nonstop from the moment we pulled in. "This used to be the Days Inn," she said.

Marcos just rolled his eyes at her, making her shut up. Then he said, "Cuz, I can't do this no more!"

Papa ignored him and everyone else. This time, he got out and went inside with Monica to get the room. The van was silent until her return. I tried to smoke a cigarette, but I couldn't take the smoke. I tossed it out the door of the van that sat open. People were walking around everywhere having fun. I wished I wasn't beat up, I might have been able to enjoy myself. That wasn't the case.

Nobody spoke to me when Monica and Papa finally came back to the van—I guess because they all had to share a room together upstairs, while Papa and I had a bungalow by the pool around the back of the hotel. I didn't complain. Monica was sick about my promotion. Her eye was still visibly black. What she didn't know while she kept smacking her lips is that I couldn't care less about my corner office with the view. I was still a ho, and from what I'd seen so far, he might send me out to the track beat-up. For all I cared, she could have him, be his bottom bitch, and lay up with him by the pool.

Papa was trying to be sweet, but him helping me walk by holding me up only added to the injury. I almost collapsed walking through the alley past the adjoining bar around the back to our room. The lobby was too crowded to walk through, so again I had to go through pain and suffering to save his image. Once finally inside our room, I rushed into the bathroom to avoid facing him. The bathroom had a dirty towel, and a roach ran when I turned on the light.

Looking at myself in the mirror, I couldn't cry anymore, but the image before my eyes was so dreadful, I would rather slit my wrist than try to put on makeup. My bottom lip was cut through from my teeth, my eyes were nearly swollen shut, my ear was bleeding from my earring getting snatched out, and a patch of my hair was pulled out from the side of my head.

I came back out of the bathroom, shutting the door behind myself— but before I did, I made a promise to never again look at myself in the mirror.

"Hey there, beautiful!" he lied to me as soon as I came into the room. He avoided eye contact, and I could understand why. *I* didn't want to look at me. How could he?

I just stood there staring at him. I demanded his attention. He finally looked but still didn't say anything to me. *Sorry* would be the last word to leave his mouth to me, because if I had a gun, I would have shot him through his mouth.

Satisfied that he felt my pain, I laid across the bed. It wasn't a king-size or anything. The room was far from nice. The smell of mildew filled up my nose as I took in the comforter.

"Baby!" he said, jumping to pull the blankets so I could lie on top of the sheets. "Them top comforters be all fucked on. Ain't no telling whose nut you just laid that pretty face of yours in."

I couldn't believe my ears. This man was the devil. I said, "Please leave me alone!"

He smiled, glad to get a response from me. "I hate to sound crazy, but drama turns me on," he said and then immediately pulled his dick out, and by golly, he was hard as a rock.

"You are sick," I told him, this time really believing the words I could barely speak.

"How?" he asked, leaning over the bed, putting his dick all on my closed lips, rubbing it on top of my busted lip. "You got my pimp juices flowing."

The thought of biting his dick off briefly crossed my mind. I wished it was that easy, but I knew it was not. Instead, I opened my bloody mouth up as much as I could, which didn't matter. Papa did the honors when he forced my mouth open around his dick. Then he humped my face and it hurt, bad. I was moaning not from pleasure but from pain, which I found out at an early age were one and the same. Papa knew it too, so he ripped off my panties and fucked me as hard as he could. The amount of blood left on the sheets was enough to fill up a tub of water. It was my baby, I knew it. He aborted my unborn child himself. To hell with a doctor. The pimp juice of his gave both life and death. I wasn't sure I'd ever dreamed or had a nightmare so surreal as this game.

After he saw the puddle of blood, he picked me up and carried me into the bathroom. He sat me on the toilet while he turned the water on. The shower curtain was stained around the bottom and had a brownish color to it just like the tub.

Then he told me, "Use the bathroom."

"I don't have to," I said.

He bent down and took his hand and pushed my stomach in and said, "Push like you doing number two."

I did. A huge gushing sound came out of my pussy. There was intense cramping pain, but still a relief of release. I looked down between my legs and saw blood clots and a bunch of blood. The sight brought a few tears to my eyes that I couldn't release. They stayed in. Papa looked sad but also like this wasn't the first time he had done something like this.

When he helped me up and into the shower, a huge weight was lifted off my chest. I had miscarried my baby, and unlike so many other women out there, I had my man to share the moment with.

"It's cold!" I shivered at the first step inside. I looked down and was still dripping blood.

He adjusted the temperature and then jumped in with me. I looked at him totally naked for the first time. Every time we'd had sex before, his pants were around his ankles. Now looking at his pot belly, his scars, his nappy pubic hair, I saw he was real. The blood that was dried up on him washed away along with mine down the rusted drain.

Papa washed me up first and then gave the same towel to me, turning his back to me for me to wash him up. I did. I used the same strictly business approach to wash his back as he used to wash mine.

"You hungry?" he asked me. He was tipping the bellboy who brought us our things. The bellboy was African and young.

"Yes," I shivered. I was cold, dizzy, and weak.

He tossed me a plastic bag that I opened up and dumped out on the bed. It was a lace wig, some cheap sunglasses, makeup, hair ties, a pair of scissors, and hair glue. I looked at him and just watched as he stood in a dirty towel going through Mama's suitcase, where he took out the same one-piece Prada silk outfit she had on the night before and laid them out next to me on the bed along with her red-bottom heels.

He opened up the lock on his Burberry carry-on bag and slung it open, dumping it onto the bed next to me. There was so much money that I covered my bottom lip with my hand.

"Count this up and use them hair ties to bundle them up in thousand-dollar stacks. The ones already wrapped are a gee apiece," he said. I did as I was told. After I finished counting up the money, there was thirty-one thousand in bundles and around seven hundred left over. Seeing this, Papa threw his slacks over to me and said, "Put what's left over with the money in my pocket."

This crazy pimp knew how to stack up some money. Thirty thousand is more than most people make in a year, let alone a few weeks. Then who gets a bitch pregnant and travels all over the United States in that amount of time? A pimp!

Soon as I finished counting up the money, I put a makeup pad in and finished getting dressed. Then I broke my promise and used the room mirror to put on my front lace.

Growing up, I used to help my mother put wigs on and used to get dolled up in her wigs when she wasn't around. That was my favorite thing to do. I always behaved myself when my daddy would force me. It seemed like he only messed with me when I wore mommy's wigs. Maybe in some sick way, that's why I wore them. Maybe I wanted some attention? His attention.

Looking more at myself with my jet-black mushroom style, with a long back piece that came down to my hood on the back of Mama's one-piece, I put on my makeup and my glasses and couldn't even tell how badly I was beat up. I couldn't see in the dark, either.

"Damn, you are sexy," Papa said. He was also dressed up in black True Religion jeans, a black V-neck sweatshirt with the sleeves rolled up, and some black boat shoes.

I blushed, not because he said I looked good, but because I believed him. I said, "What do you want me to do with this money?"

"Put it in the safe and use Carlton's birthday for the lock code," he said fluently, like he'd had it planned all day.

After I got everything together, we went up to get Red and Monica so they could go out to eat with us. Papa had me call Mr. Chow across the parking lot at the W to set us up a secluded table. I had heard stories about Mr. Chow, so going there was exciting.

Soon as I walked into the room behind Papa, all the bitches' mouths dropped. Most likely it was Mama's outfit, but nobody could say that.

"You . . . you . . . you look nice," Red finally blurted out.

"You look nice too!" I told her. She wore a black dress and some black stilettos.

Monica, on the other hand, walked up and hugged me. That surprised me. I was expecting her to be a bitch, but she was happy for me. She took me out to the balcony to smoke a cigarette.

"You okay?" she asked me.

I look out of the room at the dark Atlantic Ocean. It roared similar to the way it did in Atlantic City. The view was captivating. "Yes," I said.

"We got to stick together," she said.

The first thought that came to mind was when Mama told me to never take sides against Papa. I then thought about how Liz tried to play me close just to get me alone so she could run off to Papa; but then I remembered Story telling me to watch all these pink-toes. I said, "I already chose! Look where it got me!"

Monica didn't say anything else to me. She finished smoking and then left me as if I didn't matter. I didn't. None of these bitches were going to choose me over Papa. I guess I didn't respond the way she liked.

Walking across the parking lot to the W was like trying to cross the desert. It seemed far, but it wasn't as bad as it seemed. The whole time we walked, Papa held my arm up in his like I was his date. The girls walked at a distance the way children walk ahead with their family.

Every face inside the W was on is. The crowd was very upscale, the music in the lobby was hip Mediterranean, and the glass door to enter Mr. Chow was to the left. Papa led the way. This was his crowd. These people were our clients. They could afford to have a nice time. Not many people still can.

"Is there anything you would like to drink?" the waitress asked. She was young and cute, and she had her eyes on Papa only.

He answered, "Cristal."

"Okay, here's your menu. I will be right back with that. Enjoy!"

I looked around at the crowd. From our secluded table, I could see we stood out. Then I looked around our table. The faces, the positions had changed so much, so fast, that it seemed unreal. Was this life? How? Where was Mama? What was Liz doing?

The only thing I liked was the lettuce-wrapped pork that we dipped in this soy ginger sauce. The Cristal was nice too, but extra. The whole experience had a purpose, and from the looks on all of our faces it worked. We understood what had to be done to be able to feed our bodies these meals. He knew how to get a bitch to open her mind up to her surroundings.

"If you don't want to work tonight to heal up, I understand," Papa said.

Everybody smacked their lips. Monica even choked on her food. Then she said, "That's a bunch of bullshit!"

I lifted my hand up to stop the madness before it began. Story was by far my biggest fan. Even though she never said it, she showed it. I was like her black dog. There were times when there were three or four white girls and only two of us, but now I stood at the head of the table, next to Papa. Beat up or not, that was what the game was about.

"I wouldn't ever not work," I said. Then I looked at Monica and said to him, "What makes me different from anyone else?"

That was the second time I ever saw a genuine smile on Papa's face. He wasn't looking at me but at Monica. Then he said, "I want you two to go to the Fontainebleu to the club Liv. Story, you and Red work Ocean Boulevard. Go to the Clevelander, then the New Cafe, and then cross over to Washington Avenue and go up to SoBe Live.

"Okay!" Story said, excited.

"SoBe Live?" Red asked. "That's all white people."

Story grabbed her hand, and I knew then that they would make a good team.

"Stay off 14th and Collins. That's snatch-a-ho now. Stay away from the taco place and the Deuce bar, and call me every hour."

After Papa gave us our orders, he handed us all a hundred dollars apiece and told us to go. Without hesitation, we all got up. Papa didn't look up from the table. He was now drinking a Top Shelf Margarita.

The waitress smiled at us as we walked away, leaving him behind. It didn't take her any time to make her way over to his table. I looked back over my shoulder as I went through the revolving doors but forced myself to not stare.

Out in front of the hotel there were limos, taxis, and exotic cars lined up. The club that was connected to the hotel had a small line out front. Monica went straight to work. She already had the attention of a couple of guys. Story and Red walked off the opposite way down Collins.

I could no longer feel sorry for myself. Papa wasn't there to hold me up anymore, so I looked around for a minute before taking my first step. Monica joined me, and before long, we were inside a cab heading up Collins to the Fountainebleu. The car was silent. Monica and I hadn't been seeing eye to eye lately, and other than the night in Atlantic City, we hadn't worked together before. It wasn't about competing or outdoing each other, or was it? Who cared? I sure as hell did not. I had a plan of my own. I had a trick for all of them.

CHAPTER 21

It was eight a.m. and I laid like I had just woken up, but the truth was that I hadn't gone to sleep at all. We'd come upstairs to his room after the club let out. He was this rich real-estate developer. He was white but claimed to be married to some fat black chick. For the most part he was cool, other than the fact that he hadn't paid me. We hadn't had sex either, which really didn't make a difference. Time is money, that's part of the rules. It's not my fault that after seeing my bruised and beat-up body, he refused to have sex with me. He still held me but was turned off sexually.

"You up?" I asked him. I had forgotten his name.

"Yeah," he whispered back. Was he not asleep either? "You need a cab?"

"I don't know. Do I?" I asked. I tried to spunk up, but he knew better. "You trying to get rid of me?"

"Look, honey," he said, and the moment he opened his mouth, I knew some bullshit was to follow. I also knew it was my fault I didn't get my money up front. He said, "I don't do pimps!"

"You don't do pimps?" I repeated.

"No, I don't!" he assured. Then he got up and, still fully dressed, made his way to the phone. "I think it's best if you just leave."

"You owe me a thousand dollars for last night!" I said.

He laughed and then put the phone back down and said, "Are you crazy? I wouldn't give you the cab fare if I didn't want you the hell off the property!"

"You either give me my money, or I will run to the lobby and tell the hotel to call the cops because you beat me and raped me," I said. I couldn't believe the words that came out of my own mouth. Hell, it was worth a try.

"You little bitch!"

130

"Your mama!" I said, gathering my things.

He looked me up and down and then went into the pockets of his pants, pulled out his black leather wallet, flung three hundred-dollar bills on the bed, and said, "It's all I got!"

I snatched the money up and left. It was better than nothing. Besides, Papa hadn't texted or called my phone all night long. This was the first time he'd ever done a thing like that.

I hopped in the first cab and made my way down to the hotel. When I pulled up front, I saw there were a few Miami Beach police cars up on the ramp and on the street. The hotel was big, so at first it never crossed my mind what this could be, but then I saw Red in the back of the first cruiser.

"Keep going, please!" I yelled to the cabdriver. He was Jamaican, with the Jamaican flag dangling from the rearview mirror. He wore dreadlocks in his hair and spoke in a way that was hard to understand.

"You say 21st and Collins," he yelled.

"Here," I yelled back, throwing a hundred-dollar bill up front. "I need you to pull into the alley on side of the bar."

"Okay," he said, happy now to be overpaid. "You want I can wait?"

"Yes," I said as we pulled into the back.

I jumped out of the cab once I saw the coast was clear. I walked around to our room. It was empty. Using my key, I went inside, and from the looks of things, it was just how Papa and I had left it.

Moving fast, I ran straight for the safe, using my son's birthday to unlock it, and the bag was still there, full of money. I grabbed it along with a few of my things and Papa's laptop—then, as if by a split second, I made my way out to the cab just as the Miami vice squad came out of the hotel back door and ran straight for the room.

My heart skipped a beat. I had to keep my composure. One of the officers with tattoos and spiked hair stopped and gave me a long stare as I loaded my bags in the trunk of the cab. He looked like he was going to grab me at first, but he was blocked by the fence. He turned and walked away, still looking back as we drove off.

"That was close," the driver said to me. "Where from here?"

"Just take me to the bus station!" I said.

"The bus station? You mean the airport? Nobody takes buses anymore," he joked. "Tell you what, I can take you to the Fort Lauderdale bus station at no extra charge."

"Okay, go!" I said. "Fort Lauderdale bus station."

He turned off the meter, and before you knew it, we were speeding up the I-95 in the fast lane. He drove like a maniac. I was sleepy, and the fact that I hadn't been to sleep in days had me a bit delusional. The harder I tried to keep my eyes open, the heavier they began to feel.

I was awakened by my phone ringing; it was Monica.

"Bitch, where you at?" she yelled into phone hysterically. "They got Daddy, Story, and Red!"

"Why?" I asked, not really caring. I knew I shouldn't have answered my phone anyway.

"Red is only seventeen!" she said.

"What?"

"Yes, the bitch got busted by the Vice and told on everybody!"

"How do you know this?" I asked.

"The bellboy at the hotel told me what happened. They tore the rooms up. All our bags are being held for us, but they made me leave the premises for now," she said, sounding like she was crying. "Where the fuck are you?"

I waited for a second or so before I answered her. It took everything inside not to tell her that I was on my way to the bus station with all the money, ready to go home. Then I said, "I am still with my date. We are at the bank."

"Bitch, come get me!" she demanded. Deep down, I took her words to heart. This bitch needed me, my team needed me.

"Turn around," I demanded.

The driver looked disappointed in me, but he did what I asked. Before long, we were meeting back up with Monica on 18th and Collins at the San Juan Hotel. I gave the driver another hundred, and he became my personal driver.

Monica panicked and already had a room when I got there, and when she saw me coming into the room with my bags, she frowned. Then she saw I had Papa's money bag and attacked me, squeezing me, finally happy to see me.

"How did you?" she asked me. Then she looked again at me and realized she already knew the answer.

"What happened?" I asked to change the story.

"I told you," she said, getting smart.

"Look, we got to figure all this out!"

"I already got all this figured out," she said again with another frown.

"It wasn't like that," I said.

"What was it like?" she asked, now having a seat, her eyes on the money bag.

I threw it at her as hard as I could and said, *"I don't want this! Look at me, bitch!"*

"Bitch, look at me!" she said, and she was right. *"That was money from us all. You had no right to take that."*

"I am sorry!" I cried. *"You are right, I shouldn't have, but what better would it have been if the police would've taken it?"*

"They didn't! You did!" she reminded me, and then she tossed the money back to me. *"But you came back! I do understand how you feel."*

I couldn't believe my ears. She would've done the same thing. She was all I had right now.

I said, *"You going to bond them out?"*

"Story will be released with no bond, but Papa's bond is fifteen thousand—ten for promoting prostituting and five for renting the place to be used for prostitution," she said. *"I found a bail bondsmen that will get him out, but he said it will take a few hours before he can because he is up in Boca Raton."*

"Damn! You have been on top of it!" I said.

"Bitch, I was getting my daddy out of there even if I had to rob a bank," she laughed.

"Your crazy ass would be in there with him if you did some shit like that," I said, laughing too.

"How much money is here?" she asked.

"Thirty thousand."

"Damn! Bitch, what was you going to do with all that money?"

"I have no idea," I said.

I called for my driver, Ramell, to come back to the hotel to pick Monica up so she could go get her things from the other hotel. She left the money bag next to me and gave me a kiss on the cheek before leaving.

I was too sleepy to stay up any longer. My feet were cut around my ankles from Mama's shoes. As expensive as they were, they hurt like hell. Papa was right—they were large shoes to fill.

After I'd closed my eyes for what seemed like a full hour, Monica was back with her bags. The room had three beds inside it, which at first was weird, but it worked out fine. Our room was right next to the pool, separated by a door with a key to lock us in or out. It was an old-fashioned hotel, but nice.

"You coming?" she asked me. She was sitting in the bed next to me counting out the fifteen thousand to bond Papa out.

I didn't answer. I just got up and went to the bathroom. The blood was gone, which was a relief; however, I was still stuck with what-ifs. Was my unborn baby a boy or a girl?

I carried that thought clear to the Dade County Jail. We rode in silence as usual, other than the way Monica talked to me, almost with respect. I have no clue if she respected me for having the courage to leave or for having the love for the game to come back.

Ramell never complained or turned on the meter from the moment we stepped into the car. He was cool. Maybe he liked the excitement surrounding me so far. I couldn't lie, he wasn't cute, or sweet, or even cool, but I felt like I could trust him.

Story came out first. As soon as she saw us, she ran to the car. She was still crying, and from the looks of it, she had been crying the entire time.

"What happened?" I asked her. She got into the cab and squeezed me so hard it hurt.

"That bitch got us caught up!" she yelled.

"How?"

"Because she got dumb drunk and acted like a fool. The bitch was so out of control that she gave my number to the undercover Miami Vice officers."

"Then what happened to Papa?" I asked.

"When they came to the room to do a date with us, they found out that the room was in Papa's name. So after they locked us both up, they used my phone and found the name Daddy in it and texted him to come to the room to help me get this trick that wouldn't pay me!"

I couldn't believe my ears. The first thought in my mind was, what if I had called Papa to help me with my date earlier? Then I asked, "Red was a minor?"

"Yes, this bitch is seventeen and had a fake ID. They tried to charge him with her being a minor but couldn't. I guess because she had a fake ID and said he had no clue how old she was."

"Where is Marcos?" Monica asked.

"Papa sent him to Tampa to pick up Mama and his girlfriend, Lisa. I guess they together and Lisa ready to work."

Hearing Story mention Mama made my stomach turn inside out. I missed her on one hand, but then again, I really wasn't ready to go through all that shit again.

"Daddy!" Monica yelled, seeing him come out of the jail. He was putting on his belt as he walked. She jumped out first and ran up to him.

"Watch it, bitch!" he said, blushing. Then he held his arms out and she hugged him.

I stayed inside the cab. Story got out too. For some reason, I couldn't face him. He paid me no mind either.

They walked around to the back of the jail to pick up his property. I just sat in the cab. It was getting late. The burrito van was packing up as well . . .

Hearing the long loud sound of a horn and feeling a sudden jerk, I jumped up. Dazed and confused, I looked around at my surroundings and noticed we were just arriving at the Fort Lauderdale Greyhound station. The money bag was still next to me in the back of the cab along with my phone, which was powered off. Papa would be looking for me and his money, but until then, I was thirty thousand dollars richer.

I remember when Mama asked me in Atlantic City if I knew how much money I'd made since I chose Papa, and honestly I didn't know; but I knew one thing for sure, thirty thousand was a good enough number for me. It was wrong to leave them like that, especially in trouble, but what was the difference in getting left alone with no shoes or anything?

The driver was happy with the money I'd paid him so far. He never did ask for any more money and wouldn't accept the tip I tried to give him.

Once inside the airport, I turned my phone on real quick to see if I had any missed calls or texts, and to my surprise there were none. There wasn't anybody there but me. I went into the restroom and changed into some leggings and flip flops. I left the wig on, put on one of Papa's T-shirts, and looked at myself in the mirror. I smiled.

Looking at myself this time, with smeared makeup, crusted up blood under my lip, the dark shadow around my eye, I looked good. For the first time, I liked the way I looked. I looked strong.

"Where to?" the black lady behind the desk asked me with a fake smile.

I looked at all the destinations I could choose from. With the money I had, I could choose anywhere. Tampa was a possibility. I could see my sister. That would be nice, but she wouldn't know how to make me feel better about myself. I needed more than that.

Then I saw Delaware and thought about Sam. He was sweet to me and the only man who ever made love to me. He treated me like a lady, not like the hooker that I portrayed myself to be. Going closer to him seemed ideal. But then, what if I had to be his number two? That was a nightmare I would hate to relive.

Then there was Chicago! It might sound weird, but the first black date I ever did still texted me every night before he went to bed. He still checked on me. I knew that I could find love there with him, but is love what I really needed? Especially from a stranger?

"South Bend, Indiana," I told the lady. Of all the places I needed to go, it was home. Of any place I was going to find love, it was going to be there.

The lady smiled again as she typed away on the keys and handed me my printout. There was something about the lady that made my heart warm. She had a wig on like me, looked to have been very pretty in her day, and had a permanent scar on her cheek.

I wondered if she had been through the game like me. I wondered how many other women had been through even half of what I'd been through in these couple months.

Lucky for me, my bus was ready to leave. It helped because I wanted to text and check on Papa so bad. Instead, I looked at my screen, tossed the phone in the trash, and headed home, vowing to never look back.

The End

Epilogue

Jackie was so pretty. I almost cried when she picked us up from the bus station. Carlton gave her a hug, which was sweet, because ever since my attorney got the state to grant me custody of him, funniest thing was that he talked so good and proper.

"Mama?" he asked me. "Is this Tee-Tee?"

"Yes, Carlton! That's your Tee-Tee."

"Love you, Tee-Tee!" he said. He told everybody he loved them. Even strangers.

"Mama?"

"Yes, Carlton?"

"Love you!" he said. It was weird being in Tampa again. Hearing the word *Mama* made me think of another Mama. It had been over a year since I had seen or heard from any of them. Once I got custody of Carlton, I'd moved to Indianapolis, Indiana, hoping to get away.

In the back of my mind, I knew one day I would run into Papa again. Actually, I wouldn't mind seeing him again. I missed him, but not just him. I missed the game!